THE WORST DAY EVER!

Aliens! Spaceships!
Poo-scented
air fresheners!

JAMES BISHOP
ILLUSTRATED BY FAY AUSTIN

h HODDER

HODDER CHILDREN'S BOOKS

First published in Great Britain in 2022 by Hodder & Stoughton

1 3 5 7 9 10 8 6 4 2

A CIP catalogue record for this book
is available from the British Library.

MIX
Paper from
responsible sources
FSC® C104740

ISBN 978 1 444 95097 7

Printed and bound in Great Britain by
Clays Ltd, Elcograf S.p.A.

The paper and board used in this book
are made from wood from responsible sources.

Hodder Children's Books
An imprint of
Hachette Children's Group
Part of Hodder & Stoughton Ltd
Carmelite House
50 Victoria Embankment
London EC4Y 0DZ

An Hachette UK Company
www.hachette.co.uk

www.hachettechildrens.co.uk

This book is for a brilliant, cheeky little Chunka Dunk from planet Chardog and a funny, caring Floo Floo, both of which happen to now live on a blue and green planet I like to call home.
And their mummy.

CONTENTS

K'POW!

I opened the door of my spaceship, stepped out and landed with a THUD on the cold, hard ground of Planet K'POW. (I had forgotten to lower the steps of my ship. Not my finest moment, I'll admit!)

I placed my hand on the side of my head. Yep ... the bald patch was still there. There's something you need to know about me: I take particular pride in my hair. It's wavy, well conditioned and smells of digestive biscuits. It's also electric blue, just like my body, which is fairly slim, pretty tall and otherwise unremarkable really. BUT my hair is perfect, you hear me? PERFECT!

Less so when there's a chunk missing, burnt off

during an unfortunate accident. Now it's patchy and smells like burnt cheesecake. I'll be honest, it's up there with the worst thing to ever happen to me. My poor, INCREDIBLE hair …

I pretended I was looking for something on the ground and that I had totally meant to fall out of my spaceship to search for it. Thankfully no one had seen my embarrassing tumble, so I got up, dusted myself off and took in my surroundings. I was in a spaceship park.

One, two … skip a few, seventy-two spaceships! Wowzers, this is a pretty popular hairdresser's! I thought. Good, a popular hairdresser's was surely a good hairdresser's, and I needed the number-one recommended salon in the Universe on Spaceadvisor.

I looked past the spaceships to the row of shops behind and there in the middle, right between an ice cream shop called Lick and a bar called Glug, I found what I was looking for.

'YESSS!' I exclaimed, punching the air. I had made it to The Chop. If anyone can fix my hair, it'd be the hairdressers in that salon. Getting my hair fixed wasn't the only reason I was here, of course, but I'll be honest, fixing my locks was very much my first priority.

'Welcome to The Chop,' said a bright-red alien with a beaming smile, as I walked through the door. They took my coat and hung it on the coat rack in the corner. 'Please, take a seat,' they said, jiggling their jelly arm in the direction of the waiting area. It's probably worth mentioning that the native inhabitants of Planet K'POW were large, gelatinous blobs. Imagine a really large jelly on a plate, stick on a couple of jelly arms and big googly eyes, then remove the plate.

'Whoaaaaaaaaaaa, that's NOT my hair!' screamed an alien who was having their hair cut. If you have never been to an intergalactic hairdresser's, you should know that it's quite common to hear these words being screamed loudly. Aliens come in all shapes and sizes and what might look like hair to one alien could be the most prized possession of another.

The hairdresser had been chopping away at a green alien that looked like it was made of rock. On the side of its head there was mould that was, apparently, NOT its hair, as the scream would suggest.

I stopped in my tracks for a moment when I saw the hairdresser. She was one of the most strikingly beautiful aliens I had ever seen, and for the first time in my life I had hair envy! OK, the second time, as my obsession with hair had begun the day my parents gave me a poster of the Queen of the Universe, Tanka Tanka Woo Woo. Her hair was like a never-ending purple waterfall that seemed to flow across her head. It was truly magnificent and impossible, but this hairdresser's hair was certainly a close second.

Besides her beauty she stood out in another way, as she was the only hairdresser who wasn't a gelatinous blob. Far from it; she was a perfect shade of violet, with six arms that glided through the air in perfect sync. Her eyes sparkled like diamonds and her tongue was a fiery red, but her hair ... It was a brilliant gold that shone like twenty-four carrots.* It wrapped around her body like a helter-skelter, hovering just above the ground at the

* On Planet Iris, they spent decades searching for the brightest light in the Universe. After considerable testing, they realised that if you bound together twenty-four carrots, covered them in tin foil and shot them into the nearest sun, it would provide you with the brightest light of all, hence the phrase 'shone like twenty-four carrots'. It's worth pointing out that this has been disputed by many of the Universe's leading scientists, who say that the people of Iris simply got bored of all the testing, shot a bunch of carrots into the sun and said, 'That'll do.'

bottom. It was stunning.

She had an air of authority about her too, as after the scream of the green rock alien she simply shrugged her shoulders and chopped at the grass that was growing directly on top of its head as if nothing had happened.

'Thank you, Heather,' said the green rock, who seemed happy with this, so the grass must have been its hair.

Meanwhile, in the waiting area, I couldn't help but overhear two blobs. 'I tell you, Flobble, I have had the Worst. Day. EVER,' said a purple blob on my right.

'You think YOU had a bad day, Blurgh?' said the orange blob opposite. 'Let me tell you, mine was MUCH worse.'

Here's the thing. I have heard this conversation a thousand times before, and it always goes the same way.

'I fell over in a puddle,' said Flobble.

'I stood up on the bus and my jelly bum made a noise and everyone thought I'd farted, but I swear

I didn't!' said Blurgh. 'And I lost my wallet,' they continued.

'I lost my car,' replied Flobble.

'I lost my house,' said Blurgh. Now the game of one-upmanship had really begun. 'And I really DID fart on that bus!'

This was getting ridiculous. 'Amateurs!' I shouted. 'You don't know the first thing about having a bad day!' The room fell into a stunned silence. I wouldn't normally shout like this, but I was having a pretty kroogletastic* day myself.

'Excuse me?' said Flobble.

'What are you, some kind of expert on bad days?' said Blurgh. 'Although you do smell like burnt cheesecake, so I can understand that you're not exactly having the best day ever.'

'I quite like burnt cheesecake,' said Flobble, giving me a big sniff.

'Who died and made you king of bad days, huh?' added Blurgh, turning towards me.

'Well, I wouldn't say I was the KING,' I said, 'although

---

* Although 'kroogletastic' sounds incredibly positive, it actually has the opposite meaning: everything is awful. It comes from a planet where everyone always smiles and talks really enthusiastically about everything, even if they are having the worst day ever!

I am technically a prince and therefore one day will be a king, and I am an expert on bad days, so I guess in the future they could theoretically end up calling me the King of Bad Days, the same way they called the ruler of Planet Connecto the King of the Web, because he was the only one who was able to fix the Internet when the little light on the router went red. So I guess due to my experience of witnessing the worst days in the entire Universe I COULD end up being the King of Bad Days ...'

The entire room was now looking at me as if I was mad. I'll be honest, it wasn't the first time so I ignored it as usual.

'I have a book full of stories of bad days,' I said. I reached into my bag, pulled out my hefty tome and plonked it on the table in front of me.

'Ouch!' said the table, which was unusual (for a table). It reared up, flinging the book back at me. In a panic, I batted it across the room and it hit Heather, sending each of her six arms flailing all over the place, and one pair of scissors flying through the air.

'Whoaaaaa, that's not my hair!!' screamed a new customer she was working on, as the top of their horn was chopped off. Heather regained her composure almost immediately and continued cutting the hair around the horn's stump as if nothing had happened.

The table said, 'What's wrong with you? I come in here to get a simple haircut, then you all start shouting

and someone drops a heavy book on me?! Let me tell you, this place will be getting a very bad review on Spaceadvisor.'

'I am SO sorry!' I said, immediately taking responsibility for the mishap. 'I thought you were a table,' I said to the table.

'I AM A TABLE! Have you never been to Planet Furnitureama?'

'I ... uh ... no,' I said apologetically.

'I've never been so insulted. Come along, Gerald,' said the table, gesturing towards the coat rack in the corner as she stormed out.

Gerald the coat rack shuffled over. 'Sorry about my wife. She really doesn't like being mistaken for a table. I mean, she IS a table, of course, but, well ... she just doesn't like being treated like one.' He handed me my coat and followed his wife out of the door.

I suddenly remembered that the table wasn't the only casualty during the mishap. I rushed over and picked up the customer's horn from the floor and handed it to them.

'Don't worry, it grows back. Just give it two seconds.'
And sure enough, after counting to two the horn was
back, better than ever. The customer seemed happy
enough, but as I looked up I caught the eye of Heather
the hairdresser, whose diamond-eye stare seemed to be
cutting right through me. She pulled me in close to her
with two of her arms, the other four continuing to cut
hair effortlessly.

'Listen here, this is a respectable and discreet salon
where people come to get their hair sculpted in peace.'
Her tone terrified me a little, but her use of the word
'sculpted' had me VERY excited about what she could
do to my hair!

'I'm sorry ...' I began to apologise, but she drew me
in even closer.

'This is MY salon and I won't have any trouble. No
more funny business. Got it?' she said sternly. I nodded,
picked up my book and went back to my seat to await
my haircut.

Heather continued to chop away at the horned
alien's hair. A blur of hands and scissors later and they

were done. The shop sat in complete silence the entire time. It seems I wasn't the only one a little scared of Heather. The horned alien paid and left, and Heather approached the waiting area.

'So ... you were about to tell us how you are the King of Bad Days?' she said, catching me off guard.

'Uh ...' I mumbled. I hadn't realised she'd been listening, but clearly my story had piqued her interest. 'Ah yes, I was. BUT, in order to understand why one day I'll come to be known as the King of Bad Days, you must first understand where I come from.' I cleared my throat and stood up.

'Perhaps I should start by introducing myself.

'My name is Mylan Bletzleburger and I come from a little yellow and red planet called Empathia ...'

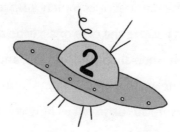

EMPATHIA

Smack bang in the middle of the Emota Galaxy, just off Hyperspace Byway 42, sits a little yellow and red planet called Empathia.

A place where the sun shines every second, of every day, throughout the year.

A place where everything smells of candyfloss and the sea tastes like cranberry juice.

A place where the birds (and trees) all sing together in perfect harmony.

A place of simple perfection.

A utopia.

My home.

Not much has been written about Empathia, so the chances are this is the first time you've heard about it. We keep ourselves to ourselves, no one visits and we don't get out much – or at all, in fact – and there is a very good reason for that.

You see, we Empathians feel everything, and I mean EVERYTHING! We are cursed with an overwhelming sense of empathy for others. Sounds weird, right? Let me explain. Imagine you stub your toe on the edge of your bed. Pretty painful, yes? But only for you. As you hop around, screaming and shouting, rubbing the sore spot as if that would help (I mean, it really doesn't, does it?!), chances are no one else really cares.

If you lived on Empathia, however, we would be hopping around with you. We have so much empathy for others that we feel exactly what those around us are feeling, from complex emotions to stubbed toes. It is EXHAUSTING!

The worst part is that our empathy sensors are super sensitive. I can pretty much feel everything that anyone is feeling across an entire planet. At the same time.

Imagine that?! It's kroogletastic!

That is why everyone back home is really nice to each other, no matter what. That way, no one ever feels bad, because if just ONE person feels bad on Empathia, EVERYONE feels bad.

As I said, I am a bit of an expert on bad days, and here's the thing about them, something I've learnt on my travels: ALL bad days begin with a stubbed toe.

I don't understand why bad days follow stubbed toes any more than I understand why the people of Planet Footrubolis greet one another by rubbing each other's feet for fifteen minutes,* but it's an indisputable fact. It's like the old saying goes:

If you hear a tale of woe,

The chances are they stubbed their toe.

I say 'old saying': I made it up (a long time ago, so I guess it's kinda old). Look at me rambling ... You want to understand what makes me such an expert on bad days, right?

I do that a lot. Ramble on and get completely distracted. It reminds me of this time I was on a planet

---

* It's really quite a strange greeting, and particularly problematic if you're running late for something and you happen to see someone you know across the street ...

made entirely of
cucumbers, came
up against an army
of robotic koalas
and I was armed with
only a banana and a
small pebble ...

I'm doing it again! You
don't want to hear about that.
You want to hear about ME, right?! Makes a change;
most people don't give two feather toads* about me,
considering my mum and dad are the King and Queen
of Empathia.

To their credit, they are the reason that Empathia
is such a lovely place to live. They have tried hard to
ensure that everyone gets on and that no one causes
any pain to anyone else. Otherwise the whole planet
would fall apart.

After years of training, as a society we reached a sort
of ... I guess you could call it ... a utopia. A heaven.
Now nobody stubs their toes, or does anything that

---

* Feather toads are, as you probably guessed, toad-like creatures covered in feathers. It's
commonly agreed across the Universe that they are pretty much the worst gift you can receive,
because they are so sticky and feathery that within seconds of holding one, you are completely
covered in their feathers, which just so happen to smell like vomit.

would cause pain to anyone else. Everyone is just really, really NICE to each other. It's pretty awesome. I guess it's the reason nobody ever leaves, I mean, what sort of idiot would EVER want to leave a utopia?! (Not much of a spoiler here, but obviously me!)

Although that's not strictly true. Two people did leave, a long, long time ago and they certainly weren't idiots because they were my parents. You see, even though they'd created the perfect world, they had one small worry. What if other worlds weren't as lucky as ours? What if other life forms in the Universe were in pain? Surely we had a duty as Empathians to help them?

But don't worry, my parents took a whizz trip around this big old Universe and reported back that everything was Zoop, Zap, Zop.* So now, no one worries. The Universe is doing pretty well. Apparently, on their travels they even met the person responsible! Tanka Tanka Woo Woo, the Queen of the Universe. They told us she does a pretty fantastic job. They even brought back a SIGNED poster of her for me that

---

* This basically means fantastic, super, amazing, etc. Zoop, Zap and Zop are AMAZING singers on Empathia, with hundreds of number-one songs. They are so good that if anything is deemed to be amazing, we just say their names. Oh, and they are trees. I mentioned that trees sing on our planet, right?!

has hung on my bedroom wall for the best part of a thousand years.

She really is a sight to behold. She has shiny metallic skin, with little specks of glitter in it that make her sparkle like a diamond; bright-yellow eyes that glare like blazing suns; she is tall and thin with a magnificently long neck that gives her a real sense of royal stature. Oh, and her hair. Her hair is AMAZING! A luxurious lavender colour, it looks more like water than hair (a difficult thing to pull off!) and splashes against her shoulders in a seamlessly never-ending waterfall.

She also has the most Zoop, Zap, Zop spaceship in the ENTIRE Universe. It's the only ship powered by ACTUAL Vansarian Tech, which is the most advanced technology ever created. It's jet black of course. All the best spaceships are jet black.

After they met with Tanka Tanka Woo Woo and were satisfied the Universe was in very good hands, they had time to stop off at a lovely little blue and green planet called Mylan for a holiday. There were lots of different creatures running around – some hairy, some not, some on land, some in water, some wore glasses, some wore contact lenses ... It was a real mixture of weird and wonderful life forms, but mostly it was the most breathtakingly beautiful place they had ever seen.

So much so that they named their only child after it.

Yep, me.

My name is Mylan Bletzleburger and this is the story of how I happened to discover the Worst Day Ever.

That's right. EVER. The worst day that ANYONE has EVER had in the entire history of the Universe. Some claim, right? But I promise you, it's the truth.

THE KING OF THE
BAD DAYS

When I had finished telling Flobble, Blurgh, Heather
and now actually the entire room about my home
on Empathia, they stared at me blankly, the blobs
wobbling slightly from side to side.

'OK, so you feel the emotions of others?' said Blurgh,
working it all out. I nodded. 'So tell me, what am I
feeling right now?'

'You are frustrated that I still haven't explained what
makes me such an expert in bad days,' I replied.

'He's right,' said Blurgh. The blobs wobbled their
heads. They were impressed. 'So tell us about that book
you're holding.'

'This book is a collection of the worst days anyone has ever had in the Universe, collected by me, Mylan Bletzleburger.'

'But why would you write that?' asked Flobble.

'I'll tell you, if you don't mind a bit of a long story.'

'I've got hair to cut,' said Heather a little impatiently, guiding a yellow blob over to her chair as she walked away. The yellow blob seemed sad to be leaving at this point in the story. 'But you may continue,' Heather added, to the delight of the yellow blob.

I smiled, sat down and told them the story of how I came to write the book. It goes a little something like this ...

I left Empathia.

The end.

I'm joking! I mean, I obviously did leave Empathia, but that CERTAINLY wasn't the end, and I'm sure I can do a better job of telling you about the beginning. Let me try again.

I grew up in the perfect world. No one was ever sad. No one was ever mad. No one was even the slightest bit unhappy. EVER.

Sounds amazing, right?!

WRONG!

Well, kinda wrong. It IS amazing but also pretty BORING. When everyone on an entire planet is concentrating SO HARD on not upsetting anyone else, EVER, there isn't a whole lot of room for fun stuff.

'Hey, let's go and play football on the field!'

'But what if someone falls over and hurts themselves?'

'Good point. Let's just sit here and talk instead.'

'But what if somebody accidentally says something that hurts someone's feelings?'

'Another good point. Let's sit here in silence!'

You can see how it would become boring pretty

quickly, right? So I ended up looking out to the stars at night and wondering, *What exactly is out there, other than a little blue and green planet and a beautiful alien with INCREDIBLE hair?*

My parents had always said, 'The Universe is doing very well, thank you very much and good day,' whenever I asked them about what was out there. That is all they would say over and over again. At an absolute push, they would add, 'Tanka Tanka Woo Woo has it all under control and isn't her hair just FANTASTIC!' because they knew it would distract me from asking any more questions (and it totally worked. Every time).

But as I grew older and reached the tender age of 345 (I know, practically still a baby, right?!), the reality that one day I would be the ruler of Empathia washed over me and I grew curious. I didn't know much, but I knew that the Universe was MASSIVE. My parents had visited just a tiny part of it, so how could they be so certain that everything was Zoop, Zap, Zop?

Yes, they had met Her Royal Highness, Queen of the Universe, but I found myself questioning their word. It's not that I didn't trust my parents – after all, Empathians by our very nature are INCREDIBLY trusting people (I didn't even come across the concept of lying until I left Empathia, and that's the truth!) – but if I was going to be the king, I felt I needed to see for myself. AND if I so happened to run into Tanka Tanka Woo Woo, get a few tips about hair maintenance and uncover the secrets behind the Vansarian Tech that powers her one-of-a-kind spaceship, so be it.

So I built a spaceship and, without telling anyone, whooshed off into space. Yes, I BUILT my own spaceship. I have two passions in this life, spaceships and hair. One day I hope to make a spaceship MADE OUT of hair.

But I'm rambling again, aren't I? What were we talking about? BAD DAYS! So, exactly how did I become an expert in them?

It's pretty simple really. I saw a lot of them. For all different life forms, on lots of different planets, but my early encounters with the Universe were very different from my parents' experience.

On Empathia there was no such thing as a bad day. But on other planets there were times when it was pretty tough to find anyone having a *good* day. I visited planet after planet and it was always the same old story. The Universe was NOT Zoop, Zap, Zop. After a short time (give or take two hundred years) of travelling, and after visiting over a thousand planets and seeing this truth, I went home and told my parents. It turns out they knew all along. They had seen it for themselves first hand.

This revelation shocked me. My parents had ... lied?! Empathians don't know how to lie; we are honest to a fault, but that also makes us pretty naive, the perfect group to *lie to* ...

Like me, my parents had learnt about lying on their travels (lots of bad days start with a lie or two) and they had lied to their own people.

I felt stupid not realising it until I had made it home. I mean, how could they not have had the same experience as me?!

They tried to explain to me that they had found

the Universe too overwhelming and they then made the difficult decision to hide the truth from the rest of Empathia. They knew that if the Empathians found out the Universe was in trouble, they would all feel compelled to leave and try to help.

They felt the Universe was past saving and even the combined efforts of all Empathians wouldn't help. So, they reasoned, why tell them when they are already living in a perfect utopia?

And it worked. Although we can feel what others are feeling, we aren't lie detectors. My parents strongly gave off the impression that all was well in the Universe and everyone believed them, including me.

I was horrified by my parents' decision, but felt completely helpless. What could I do? If I tried to tell the people of Empathia what I had witnessed, it would be my word against theirs. No one would know who to believe and it would tear apart everything my parents had built. I needed proof. Documented proof. Times, dates, planet names, detailed accounts of everything that happened, and lots of it.

So I got back into my spaceship and headed for the stars once more.

This time I would collect thousands of stories.

Stories of life forms having the worst days ever.

So many that the good people of Empathia would *have* to believe me. I would bury them in evidence.

A book full of stories that PROVED the Universe was not Zoop, Zap, Zop and it needed our help.

I began writing a book and I called it *The Worst Day Ever …*

BELCH

After I told the story of how I had come to write my book, everyone in The Chop fell silent. After a few seconds, Flobble finally spoke.

'Wow. So you really *are* an expert in bad days!'

'Yes, and I have seen some absolute shockers on my travels. You think farting on the bus is bad? Try farting into a volcano and causing an eruption.'

'Someone did that?!' said Blurgh, wobbling all over the place at the thought of it. This caused them to let out a little trump of their own, a short, squelchy, rumbly sound. They were pretty embarrassed, but it actually smelt like oranges and was rather pleasant!

'Yep, made the whole planet stink like rotten eggs,' I confirmed. 'And that's not even the worst of it.'

'Oh, really ...' Everyone shuffled a little closer to me. Heather had now put her scissors down to listen.

'I don't suppose you would like to hear a few stories?' I said. This was greeted by a sea of wobbling jelly nods.

I opened the book slowly, revealing the first page. 'This, my new friends, is the first bad day I encountered, written by me, Mylan Bletzleburger.'

It's a little-known fact, something they don't teach you in school, but the Universe stinks. I really mean it. The stench IS awful.

As soon as I had left my atmosphere, I sensed something had changed. It started off as a light stink, a bit like when you fart in the bath. There is a faint, foul aroma, but it's had to make its way through the water and the lavender bubble bath counteracts it.

For a while I thought it might be me, but after multiple spaceship baths – I held in my farts just to be sure (don't try this at home) – I smelled beautiful, like digestive biscuits and lavender. There was only one conclusion. It wasn't me, it was the Universe.

I had hoped to stumble across the little blue and green planet my parents had named me after, but the sad fact is there are billions of planets, and the chances of me finding Planet Mylan – well, it would be like trying to find a needle in a galaxy-sized haystack that was made entirely out of needles.

Instead of the mesmerisingly beautiful Mylan (the planet, not me, although when my hair is on point I'm pretty beautiful too, obviously!), I stumbled across a solid land mass with no oceans, covered in a mysterious purple haze that hovered in the sky just above the clouds. I had landed on the planet of Belch.

The first thing you need to know about Belch is the inhabitants call themselves Belchers. They release thick clouds of purple haze whenever they burp, and they burp A LOT. They burp when they laugh; they burp when they cry; they burp when they drink; they burp when they have a bath; they burp when they stand in the queue for a bus. They even burp when they burp, so every burp is a double-burper. Walk down any street in Belch and you'll witness a sea of purple clouds ascending to the sky to form part of the purple haze above. It is actually pretty beautiful until you realise what it is. I now know that the purple haze is organic and non-toxic, but I did not know that at the time and it was quite concerning.

I stood by the door of my spaceship, my finger nervously hovering over the Open button. I had never visited another planet before and I was nervous, so much so I almost forgot to BREATHE. I remembered just in time and pulled out my BREATHE dispenser. I gave the bottle a shake and removed the lid. On the other side was a small plastic circle in which a thin layer of liquid was resting. I tipped it into my mouth, blew a big bubble and when it popped, I swallowed it.

There are a MILLION different environments out there, so a BREATHE dispenser is an absolute must for every intergalactic traveller, as it helps you to breathe by converting any environment to that of your home planet. All using a simple little bubble. It's a Bubble

Respiration Enhancer, Altered To Home Environment.

I took a deep breath, then gave myself a pep talk. 'OK … OK … you can do this, Mylan. Three … two … two … two …' I got stuck on two for a while. 'Two … two … one …' I pressed the button.

No sooner had the doors opened than I was hit by an entire planet's worth of emotion. I was completely shocked. I hadn't felt pain like it before and it was completely unexpected, as my parents had of course told me that everything in the Universe was Zoop, Zap, Zop. This planet was anything but Zoop, Zap, Zop, let me tell you.

There were so many problems, it was hard to focus on just one. But after a while I managed to focus on one Belcher and feel their emotions.

I could see a young girl who had stepped up to play some sort of bat and ball game. She had swung the bat so hard and connected so perfectly with the ball that it had flown out of the park, through the sky and got lost in the purple haze. She was absolutely mortified, as the aim of this particular game was to miss the ball entirely and then do as big a burp as possible (which I could tell is exactly what she tried – and failed – to do).

Instead she hit the ball clear out of the park, hiccupped politely and fell to the ground. All the other kids were laughing at her. I felt her pain as if I was living the moment myself.

Then I lost focus on her, and the rest of the planet's troubles washed over me like a tsunami. I could hear a boy crying because he had been stuck in traffic on the way home from school and had missed his favourite TV show. The worst part? Belch was a planet without the technology to record TV. On the opposite side of the planet there was a woman who had climbed a tree to help get a cat down, only to get stuck up there herself. There was a bunch of kids waiting anxiously to do some sort of exam, but every single one of them had stupidly forgotten to bring a pen! Finally I felt the utter despair of a child who had been singing to themselves on the toilet and when they left the cubicle they were greeted by cheering and clapping from fifteen other Belchers.

This was just a little taster of what I felt, all mixed in

with a thousand other problems I couldn't focus on. I began sobbing uncontrollably and slammed the door shut in defeat.

At that moment, I realised I had only two options: head back to Empathia and tell my parents what I had briefly felt on this one planet, or stay and fight. And it would be a fight, of that I was sure. A fight to regain control of my emotions. To not feel overwhelmed. In the end, I was so interested in this new planet and what it could teach me about the Universe that I knew I had to stay. I took a deep breath, opened the door again and let the planet of Belch wash over me.

Over time, I found that if I concentrated really hard I could tune in to just one person's troubles and block the others out. It was tough, mentally exhausting and I cried A LOT, but it was possible. On Planet Belch, I ended up focusing on a Belcher called Bungaloopa.

First thing one morning I was standing outside my ship, when all of a sudden I felt a dull ache in the big toe of my left foot. It felt as if I had just stubbed it on the side of my bed, but I hadn't.

It's hard to explain, but when I closed my eyes and focused on the throbbing, it was like I could see the person in pain as clear as day. On this occasion I could see a young Belcher hopping around their bedroom screaming, burping and clutching her toe.

'OUCH! ARGH! Why me? Why *today*?!' screamed Bungaloopa. 'Could this day get any worse already?!' She then burped seventeen times in a row. I could hardly see her through the haze.

I followed her for the day. At lunch she was complaining to her friend that her mum had forgotten to put jaloona berries – little red and blue berries with a black stalk – in her jaloona berry sandwich. Now, I'm no expert on the jaloona berry sandwich, but I'm pretty sure that the jaloona berry is a key ingredient.

Her friend had some in her lunchbox but refused to give any of them to Bungaloopa, which made her sad (and me, of course; I'm sure you're getting how this works by now, right?). It just so happened that the bush I was hiding behind had these berries on them! *Perfect. I will help her out*, I thought.

On the wall in the entrance to the school was a big lever with the word 'fire' written by it. I pulled it, and everyone started screaming, which in between burps was a very strange sound indeed. I was hit by a wave of panic from everyone as they ran out, assuming that the school was on fire. *They really need to do more fire tests*, I thought, then headed over to the abandoned sandwich and dropped a few jaloona berries in.

Then I saw the actual fire. How was I supposed to know that on Planet Belch, fire drills are done with real fires! By pulling the lever that said 'fire', I had started a fire. I mean, that's both extremely dangerous and stupid (but as I travelled the Universe, I realised it's strangely common practice on many planets).

I had made poor Bungaloopa feel scared, which made me sad, but her smile when she saw her fully loaded jaloona berry sandwich on her return made up for it. Until she took a bite. Turns out they weren't jaloona berries, they were baloona berries (which in my defence look EXACTLY the same!), which make Belchers inflate and float into the sky. Luckily, as

Bungaloopa rose up from the ground a teacher caught her and took her inside and she spent the rest of the day trying to do her work on the ceiling.

I returned to my spaceship feeling deflated, which is exactly how Bungaloopa felt (emotionally deflated that is. It took three days for her to physically deflate. Baloona berries are strong!).

TALKING CHOP

I closed my book and looked round the salon.

'Wow! What a story! Bungaloopa's baloona berry blunder, bloomin' brilliant!' said Blurgh.

'You can say that again!' said Flobble.

'I don't think I can, actually,' replied Blurgh.

'The things you must have seen! The name's Flobble. Always nice to meet a fellow intergalactic traveller,' they said, going in for a bear hug. For a second it felt like I was drowning in goo. When Flobble released me I was utterly drenched (but smelt divine).

'You've been to the galaxy next door, Flobble. That hardly makes you an intergalactic traveller,' said Blurgh dismissively.

'Well, I've visited
more than one
galaxy. That counts
as intergalactic,
wouldn't you say,
Mylan?' asked Flobble.

I ignored the question as I
patted myself down, trying to get rid of the excess goo.
'Interesting name you have there. What did you say it
was again?' I asked.

'Flobble,' said Flobble. 'It's one of our planet's quirks.
Everything on Planet K'POW is named after the very
first sound it made.'

'So ... Blurgh?' I said, pointing towards the purple
blob. Blurgh wobbled his head in an enthusiastic
nod. 'A pleasure to meet you both. Wait, K'POW ...' I
mused, before saying it again with a little more gusto.
'K'POW.' I clapped my hands and mimed an explosion.
That would have been the planet's first sound as it was
created.

'Exactly,' said Flobble with a smile, seeing the penny drop.

'And this place is called ... The Chop,' I said thoughtfully. I also smiled at the thought of the ice cream shop and bar that were either side of the hairdresser's: Lick and Glug.

'Yes,' said Heather, as she pointed towards the hair on the floor without looking at it. A tiny lime blob wobbled over from the corner and began sweeping. 'Along with forty-three other hair salons on the planet. I've tried to get the name changed, but the council ignore my letters, which has left me incredibly frustrated. I don't like not being in control,' she said through gritted teeth. 'It's not something I'm used to ...' She seemed to be staring right through me again.

'I was looking for a particular hairdresser's that has come highly recommended,' I began.

Heather picked up a fancy-looking hairdryer and took a step closer to me. 'THIS is the best hairdresser's in the entire Universe,' she said boldly.

I took one look at the hairdryer and froze. It was

Vansarian Tech. I could tell just by looking at it. It was a thing of beauty, but of course it was – that technology was legendary!

Not much is known about the people of Vansaria. In fact, no one even knows where the planet of Vansaria is, but the technology they create is second to none. It's so good that, upon discovering it, the Queen of the Universe decreed that no one else could have access to it. That way she would always be one step ahead of any potential enemies, and could continue to keep the peace in the Universe.

This was the first piece of kit I had seen with my own eyes and Heather was pointing it right at me. Knowing how powerful anything made of Vansarian Tech could be, I began to sweat. A lot. When Empathians sweat, it comes out like a sprinkler. I was drenched within seconds.

Heather pushed the button on the hairdryer and in the half-second it was on, I felt an unbelievably strong gust of wind that left me bone dry. She smiled for the first time and confirmed my theory.

'Vansarian Tech, the same tech that powers the ship of—'

'Tanka Tanka Woo Woo,' I said in awe. I had never been so close to this level of technology before. The things I could do with it …

'That's Her Royal Highness, Queen of the Universe to you,' said Heather, as if speaking for the Queen herself.

'I'm sorry?' I said, almost as a question.

She nodded in acceptance. 'No other salon in the Universe has access to Vansarian-powered hairdryers, so trust me, you are in the right place,' she said forcefully.

I looked at the hairdryer one more time.

'I couldn't agree more,' I said with a smile.

'Yes, yes, we are all very impressed with your silly

little hairdryer,' said Blurgh, 'but this really is taking a long time, don't you think?'

I'm not sure who looked more offended, me or Heather.

'I'll get to you in a minute,' said Heather firmly.

'No, not that. I mean Mylan's story. We know about his parents and how they lied to keep the Empathians on his planet, and that he is writing this book to convince them that the Universe needs help, and I for one enjoyed his tale of Planet Belch, but we still don't know ANYTHING about why he is here now, or how he ended up burning off half his hair!'

'I'm so sorry, I guess I am jumping around a little,' I said, touching my hair.

'Don't apologise to that grumpy, wobbly fool. Be polite, Blurgh. Let him tell his story how he wants to,' said Heather.

I nodded politely, mouthed the words 'I'm extremely sorry' to Blurgh and got back to the story at hand.

'OK, so having confronted my parents, I set back off to collect stories from across the Universe of people having bad days, and there were bad days EVERYWHERE.'

'That must have been very tough as an Empathian, seeing all those people in pain?'

'It was, Flobble,' I said, taking a moment to reflect. 'I had to fight every instinct I had to try and help people. It hurt me greatly not to at least try and help, witnessing terrible day after terrible day, but I knew in the long run it was best for everyone. If I could convince my fellow Empathians to leave, then we could help so many more people, so I simply observed and noted down what I saw.'

I patted the book gently. 'It has been hard, but there is enough in this book to convince every Empathian on the planet to join the cause, I'm certain of it.'

'So you're on your way home?!' asked Flobble excitedly.

'Almost. I have one last thing to do ...' I said, raising my hand to the bald patch on my head.

'Ah yes, your hair. My gran always used to say you need to look your best when trying to convince an entire planet to do something. Was never quite sure exactly *why* she always said this, but turns out she might have been on to something!' said Flobble.

'So what exactly happened to your hair?' asked Blurgh.

I paused, then took a deep breath.

'I found Planet Mylan. Then I did the very thing I'd sworn not to do. I started trying to help ...'

GET OFF MY FARM!

There are many strange and wonderful planets in this vast and ever-expanding Universe.

More in fact, than you could count on one hand of a Gurglesprout from the Planet Sarpong. If you aren't familiar with this peculiar creature, it's worth knowing that Gurglesprouts have A LOT of fingers. No one knows exactly how many. Even the finest doctors in the Universe have given up while attempting to count them (one did manage to reach around the 1.4 billion mark before falling asleep, and couldn't be bothered to start over). Not even Gurglesprouts know, so if you ever meet one, don't ask them. They will just hold up all seven of their hands and say, 'This many' (they think this is hilarious).

The Planet Sarpong is, however, quite ordinary in comparison to those even in its neighbouring galaxy. Hubba Bubba 7 (NOT to be confused with Hubba Bubba 6 under any circumstances if you are visiting and want to keep your head) is made entirely out of discarded pieces of chewing gum which have, over billions of years, managed to find each other, stick together and create a world capable of hosting intelligent life. Well, 'intelligent' might be a bit of a stretch considering the life forms on the planet spend most of their lives stuck to the floor.

There is a planet where the oceans are made of milk from giant space whales; a planet where everything and everyone is edible (well, there used to be. It got eaten); a planet where toilets are alive; a planet where gravity is a culinary delicacy (as you eat it, you find yourself gently floating up, up and away out of the restaurant. All the restaurants shut down though, as no one was paying their bill); a planet where every single train and bus runs on time without fail (this is perhaps the strangest planet in the entire Universe. No one is EVER late). There is even a planet where NO ONE has ever heard of Her Royal Highness Tanka Tanka Woo Woo, the Queen of the Universe.

The fact is, the Universe is massive. I mean, really MASSIVE. Bigger than you could possibly ever imagine. Even if you were by some miracle able to comprehend the sheer size of it, that realisation would only last for a second, as the Universe is also constantly expanding.

Which brings me BACK to the story! With every planet I visited, I hoped one day to stumble across my namesake: Planet Mylan. Everywhere I went I asked people if they had ever heard of such a planet, but unfortunately no one ever had (although they all agreed it sounded lovely, a perfect holiday planet).

One day, just as my parents had done many years before, I looked down from the spaceship and saw a beautiful planet. It was blue and green and perfectly spherical. It had only one moon. It looked exactly as they had described Mylan! Could I have stumbled

47

across Mylan by sheer dumb luck?

By the time I reached Mylan I had visited more planets than I could possibly keep track of, but Mylan is hands down the most spectacular that I have ever seen. As I looked down on the green (apparently that was land) and blue (this was water, it seemed) spots from my spaceship window, I wiped a tear from my cheek, thinking about the fact I had been named after somewhere so breathtakingly magnificent.

It's part of the unwritten code of intergalactic travel that when visiting another planet you should aim for as secluded a place as possible to land your spaceship. Preferably in a field at night (if the planet has fields, of course. AND they aren't full of field piranhas, which are incredibly vicious and always hungry).

We intergalactic travellers do this so as not to scare the local inhabitants, who may never have encountered an alien species before or, even more bizarrely, think that they are entirely alone in the Universe (some planets have life forms who really are that stupid!).

I landed in a field and prepared myself to open

the door to a place I had been searching well over a thousand years for. A place I had begun to believe was a myth. My parents had told me Mylan was a planet almost as perfect as Empathia. I couldn't wait to meet all the different creatures. I opened the door with a big smile on my face …

'GET OFF MYFAR!!' screamed a fairly plain-looking creature with hair all over his chin (which is a really weird place to keep hair if you ask me). Some sort of white cloud with eyes made a BAA noise in the background. It was pretty odd.

I immediately slammed the door again then bolted it shut. Not because the creature looked like they could cause me any serious harm (despite the facial hair and angry face, it was actually kinda cute looking), but because I was on the wrong planet. I was supposed to be on Mylan, but instead it appeared I had landed on Myfar instead.

I was devastated – the planet certainly matched my parents' description. The local inhabitant looked like a pretty accurate match to the illustrations my dad had drawn of some of these alien beings, but it couldn't be the same place. Unless they had lied about this too?

BANG, BANG, BANG!

I peeked out of my window to see the cute creature banging the side of my ship with a giant fork. There must be giants on this planet that this alien has stolen cutlery from ... GIANTS! I considered leaving.

'Get off MYFAR!' he continued to shout.

'Yes, yes, get off Myfar, I understand,' I muttered, even though I didn't. Despite it not being Mylan, I was curious to learn more about this eerily similar planet. There was only one course of action: to get GLOOPED up, fast.

The gloop has a much more impressive name, but it's really long. If I remember correctly, it's something like 'Exa-Hyper-Topa-Lopa-Floo-Floo-Chunka-Dunk-Moo-Moo-Mice'. I changed the name to 'magic gloop', which over the years I've simply shortened to 'gloop'.

The gloop changes your outward appearance. You slap it on, lather it all over, and then whenever you meet any other life form, you transform into something they feel at ease with. Not physically, of course, but their perception of you changes. It's really useful if you land on a planet where the beings can't comprehend alien life, or aren't particularly welcoming (which is usually one and the same thing).

It's also useful if you land in a field full of field piranhas, who then just see you as one of them (they really are quite nippy). Gloop regularly turns you into the same species as the life form itself. That is where most people's comfort zone lies.

I glooped up as quickly as I could and headed back out of the spaceship. The banging had stopped and I couldn't see the creature anywhere. That's when it really hit me. A wave of emotion unlike anything I had experienced before.

The planet was hurting. At first, it was so overwhelming I thought it was the planet *itself* talking to me. There was simply so much pain. But it was more than that. Each of these creatures seemed to be carrying a planet's worth of problems with them at all times. It was as if I was feeling the pain of an entire galaxy, not just a single planet. I hadn't even realised it, but I had dropped to my knees in the middle of the field, tears leaking from my eyes. Then I felt something on my back.

I turned quickly and found myself face to face with the creature, who had placed their giant fork on the ground next to them and was rubbing my back. 'There, there,' it said. 'Everything will be all right,' and for a few seconds, it was. My problems seemed to wash away and I felt calm.

It was harder than usual, given the overwhelming emotion of the planet, but I managed to focus in on what this creature was feeling. It was fearful, but not of me. No, it was fearful FOR me. This creature was feeling empathy.

'Me ... Marcus ...' he said slowly while prodding his chest, as if talking to a child. I had already concluded Myfar was a particularly backward planet, and this all but confirmed it. I copied his speech to make him feel comfortable.

'Me ... Mylan ...' I said, placing my hand on my chest

and smiling. He jumped backwards in shock.

'You ... can talk?!' he said, stunned.

'Me ... talk ... you ... talk,' I said.

He shook his head. I wasn't sure if he was trying to reset himself (this is something cyborgs often do) or if he was just trying to regain his composure.

He took a deep breath and started over. 'OK. Me Marcus ... Uh ... I come in peace ...'

'Wait, isn't that my line?' I said, confused.

I could sense he was shocked. He now matched my speech pattern, talking faster.

'Yeah, sorry about that. I'm just a little flabbergasted, is all. Who'd have thought that aliens spoke the Queen's English?!'

'That's what a good TALK* will get you,' I said, before suddenly realising that Marcus shouldn't have been seeing an alien. Not if the gloop was working.

'Sorry, this is crazy! I've always wanted to meet a real-life alien!' He started dancing and jumping for joy. His joy briefly overwhelmed me and I joined in with his little dance. We bounced around, swinging our

---

* Even the most casual intergalactic traveller wouldn't travel across the Universe without at least a basic TALK (Translate All Languages Kit).

arms above our heads, clicking our heels together and clapping our hands.

Not once had someone done a dance for me before. Usually I was greeted with fear or aggression when visiting a planet not used to intergalactic travellers. We spun round and kicked out our legs and in that moment I felt true happiness. I was having a great time,

but then a series of questions popped into my head. So many questions that they all came out at once.

'Excuse me, but could you please tell me why you attacked my ship, why we're now dancing, if there are any giants on this planet, if you have ever heard of field piranhas, and, most importantly, would you mind describing what I look like, please?'

The man stopped mid-jig and looked over at me, his face and heart still filled with pure joy.

'Why, of course I can! Let me see … I attacked your ship because you landed in my crops! I'd put up big bright signs, saying "Aliens, land here!" and you just ignored them!'

'Ah, sorry about that. We don't land near lights so that we don't scare the locals,' I said apologetically.

'Never mind scaring me, I'd rather have a fright than squashed peas!' he said with a hearty chuckle. 'As for giants, not that I know of, but most folk are taller than me so I'm not the best person to ask!' He laughed even harder at this. 'Never heard of no field fish, and as for you – well, you look like a bona fide, seven-foot-tall, electric-blue alien and you're completely covered in some sort of gloop. That answer your questions?'

'Most of them,' I smiled. I guessed he was so keen to see an alien that he saw me as I really was. This was the first time the gloop had had no effect. I gave myself a sniff then licked the back of my hand. I tasted amazing, but I didn't taste of gloop. In my haste to put the gloop on I must have picked up the wrong bottle. By the taste of it, I had picked up a jar of Rofel bee honey* instead. I burst out laughing. Next thing I knew, I was rolling on the floor. When I finally came round, I noticed Marcus had copied me and was lying next to me.

'I have just one final question for you, Marcus,' I said, as our heads lay on the same patch of grass, and it was by far the most important question of all. 'Is this Planet Mylan, or Planet Myfar?' I asked.

'Well now,' he said, stroking his chin hair, which seemed to help him gather his thoughts. 'This is *my* land, and it's also *my* farm. It belongs to me, from that house you can see over there, all the way to those squashed peas underneath that there spaceship of

---

* The honey of the Rofel bees from the Planet Lol causes people to laugh uncontrollably. If you ingest too much, you can die of laughter. Luckily I had only had a small lick so I just got the giggles!

yours. The planet though, well, let me be the first to say … welcome to Planet Earth. Would you like some tea?'

Planet Earth, NOT Planet Mylan, or even Planet Myfar. Suddenly it all made sense. My parents hadn't landed here and had a wonderful holiday on a utopia like they had said. Instead, it seems they'd had a similar greeting to me, landing in some field with a farmer telling them to 'get off my LAND!' They had mistaken it for the name of the planet then named me after it.

My parents' final lie had just been unravelled before my eyes. It made sense, of course. If they had lied about every other planet, why not this one too? Even so, it hurt a whole lot more. Marcus's joy had been a really powerful feeling, but it was overwhelmed by my own feelings of sadness.

I tried to focus back in on Marcus and his refreshingly positive attitude as we walked over to his house, and on the way I considered whether or not I should change my name to Earth Bletzleburger. I concluded that was stupid, as he poured me a cup of this mysterious tea …

It tasted awful and made my lips balloon three sizes bigger because hot liquid and Empathians DO NOT work well together. Our bodies are super sensitive to warm liquid. It makes our skin inflate and does unspeakable things to our hair.

Still, I tried to be polite, made some universally accepted noises that suggested I was enjoying it and smiled (after all, the Zebullons went to war with the Xenites because a visiting Zebullon spat a mouthful of sausage out after discovering it was made from a Xenite's hair). Besides, I could feel Marcus really wanted me to like it. Making a good cup of tea seemed to hold a LOT of importance to Earthlings.

(I later found out that this 'tea' was made using old leaves and had in it excreted liquid from one of the most common animals on Earth. Revolting. Had I discovered this earlier, I may well have left the planet right there. The Earthlings were lucky I wasn't a Zebullon ...)

We sat down and Marcus asked me lots of questions about my planet and all the other planets I'd visited.

His wonder and amazement made me relive my own wonder at the Universe. He was mostly interested in alien beverages and how highly Earth tea ranked on a universal scale. I told him it was a solid nine. Marcus was happy with this, making the foolish assumption the scale was out of ten, not ten thousand (and that's me being generous!).

'I sure am glad you enjoyed your tea, Mylan,' said Marcus, completely oblivious to my disgust. 'Now, let me show you to the barn. You are more than welcome to stay there for the night,' he added, walking me over to a small shack at the back of his house. It was full of hay and had the flimsiest door I had ever seen. It was a minor miracle it was still standing (the door, that is, although the same goes for the barn).

'This is very kind of you,' I managed to say, despite my lips taking up over half of my face. 'Thank you,' I added, trying to smile at him. I could sense his bewilderment, so I wasn't successful.

'Goodnight, Mylan!' he said, then he turned and headed back to his house.

Moments after he closed the door I returned to my perfectly lovely spaceship, which was warm and cosy and WAY better than a stupid cold barn. I had travelled billions of miles across space, yet he somehow thought that a couple of hay bales would be more comfortable than a travelling home that can cross galaxies. The people of this planet really weren't very clever.

The next morning I sneaked back into the barn just before Marcus returned, this time with a whole pot of that stinking, scorching tea.

'Milk?' he asked.

'Yes, please,' I said, hoping that was the right answer (I hadn't figured out it was excreted cow liquid at that point). Marcus smiled as he poured so I assumed I had guessed right. Not that it mattered; my face had only just recovered so I had no intention of drinking it.

'So what are you going to do now – take over the world?' asked Marcus calmly, while taking a sip of tea, as if he had just asked me if I planned to visit the beach, as opposed to enslaving every single Earthling and ruling over them.

'Not today. I thought I'd get to know the place a little first,' I said. 'Don't worry, I'm joking. I'm here to observe, not to rule.' I put both my hands up, palms facing out. The universal sign of being completely harmless.

Marcus chuckled. 'Ah, like one of them scouts who takes a little look-see to see if the coast is clear?'

'I come in peace,' I said calmly. Marcus smiled as if he had known this all along.

'So what *will* you do then?' he asked.

'I'm just here to observe, Marcus. I don't get involved with the people on a planet.'

'Oh, sorry!' he said, hastily trying to take the cup of tea back off me. I was half tempted to let him, but instead I decided to explain.

'Not you, Marcus. I've really enjoyed meeting you! Usually I keep a distance though. You see, I'm writing this book ...'

I went on to tell him my story and what I was doing on Planet Earth. He blinked repeatedly as if trying to compute this information (I wondered again if he really was some sort of cyborg. They are very common in the

Universe).

Suddenly I jumped up from my seat in pain, grabbed hold of my big toe and spilt my tea (that at least was a bonus!).

'What's wrong?' said Marcus, genuinely concerned.

'Stubbed toe,' I said, hopping on one foot.

'But you were sat down right there, you were!' said Marcus. 'You can't have stubbed it.'

'Not *my* toe,' I explained, as the pain began to subside. Over the years I had managed to block out most pain directly from others, but the one thing I was tuned in to was a stubbed toe first thing in the morning, and this was a doozy. The creature who'd done it was going to have a very bad day.

'I have to go,' I said.

'I understand,' said Marcus, nodding knowingly before adding, 'Actually, I've no idea what is going on, but I wish you all the luck in the Universe.' He shook my hand, and I danced for him as was his greeting, clapping my hands, bouncing from toe to toe and waving my arms in the air, and I even threw in a cheeky little bum wiggle too. It would have been impolite not to.

I was so excited by the prospect of my adventure that I wasn't looking where I was going and stubbed my own toe as I entered my ship. I laughed at the irony of dealing with two stubbed toes.

I started the engine. I was heading to somewhere called Oxford to find the Earthling with the stubbed toe and I found myself hovering just above Chloe Harrison's house a little after 8 a.m.

STUPID FLY

My spaceship was in incognito mode and not visible to the naked eye as I hovered above Chloe's house. I landed in her garden and sneaked in through the back door.

'Shoo!' said Chloe's mum, swatting her hand towards me. This time I'd put on the correct gloop correctly. Instead of a seven-foot electric-blue alien with incredible hair entering her kitchen at breakfast time, she was seeing a fly.

I sneaked past her and stood against the wall as Chloe hopped into the kitchen.

'Hey, Mum, do we have a plaster? I— OUCH!' she

screamed, as she stubbed another toe on the kitchen table. She was now unable to hop as both feet were in pain, so she fell to the ground and held them. I did the same because it was excruciating.

'HA! HA! HA!' said Chloe's brother, who stood over her, pointing.

'What are you doing down there, Chloe?' her dad asked, casually stepping over her into the kitchen. 'Thanks for pointing her out, Harry.' He ruffled the boy's hair and made his way over to the kettle.

'I ... stubbed ... my ... toes!' Chloe exclaimed, rocking herself into an upright position. I did the same. Our feet were still zunking* painful!

As I did, I got a proper look at her family. Like Chloe, her mum was short, with pale skin and fiery-red hair. At first I was slightly worried this was yet another clone planet as mother and daughter were so similar, even down to a delicate little mole on their chins. However, I looked at Harry, and then at her dad and they were chalk and cheese.** Her brother was tall and slim with wavy jet-black hair. Her dad was round and very much lacking in the hair department.

Chloe stopped rubbing her feet, gingerly grabbed on

---

* On the Planet Zunk, the concept of exaggeration is a little misunderstood. If someone wanted to exaggerate, they would end up using the word 'really' over and over.
For example – I really, really, really, really, really, really, really, really like apples.
This became unmanageable, so instead they began to use the word 'zunking' to illustrate exactly thirty-four really's.

** Chalk and cheese is actually an Earth phrase I picked up, meaning two things that simply don't go together. This made me curious and I tried them in a sandwich once and it was actually pretty good. The phrase really should have been 'like tea and milk' or 'like old leaves and excreted cow liquid', but I doubt that will catch on.

to the kitchen table and hoisted herself up, balancing on her heels.

'Breakfast?' said her mum, completely ignoring the last couple of minutes.

'Sure, just cereal, please.'

Her mum shook some kind of hard, mini circles into a bowl and poured the same white substance I had drunk in my tea over the top. This made me curious; what was this mysterious, multipurpose liquid? I looked at the side of the carton and *that's* when I discovered what milk is. Beginning her day with a bowl full of it? Awful start to the day confirmed.

Chloe hobbled to her seat, cruising the length of the table like a toddler learning to walk. She sat down and a long, meaty, flatulent sound escaped from her bottom. Her dad and brother laughed hysterically.

'URGH, Chloe, what did YOU have for breakfast?!' said Harry, offering out a high-five to his dad, who slapped his hand in return.

'You KNOW I haven't had breakfast yet, and you KNOW that was a whoopee cushion, NOT me,' said

Chloe, pulling out a pink, semi-inflated piece of rubbery plastic from underneath her. She fiercely chucked it at her brother, who ducked just in time.

SIDE NOTE – Earthlings are utterly OBSESSED with the sounds that come out of their bottoms. They find it absolutely hilarious. These sounds are also accompanied by grotesque smells that no bubble bath could cover, and I have observed some Earthlings wafting the fart towards their nose to get a better sniff. Honestly, it's quite odd. Other than making a rather wet 'toot' sound and causing a nasty stench, their farts don't do anything of interest. Not like the inhabitants of Planet Trump, who have 24-piece symphony orchestras played entirely through their bottoms. Now, that is something to be proud of.

'Please stop putting whoopee cushions under your sister,' said Chloe's mum with a stern look that was completely undermined by Harry and her dad high-fiving again. Chloe ate a mouthful of her awful breakfast and spat it out immediately.

'URGH, MUM! The milk has gone off!' she said,

scraping at her tongue.

'Probably why your farts STINK so much!' said Harry, receiving yet another high-five from his dad. Mum looked at Dad disapprovingly.

'What? Credit where credit is due,' said Chloe's dad.

I thought Chloe had simply realised what she had put in her mouth and was as disgusted as I was. But no, it was even worse. The excreted cow liquid can turn sour. Why did these Earthlings drink it?!

Chloe hobbled over to the sink on her heels and splashed some water into her mouth. She then limped over to the fridge, pulled out a carton of orange juice and returned to her seat.

TOOOOOOOOOOT!

'HARRY!' said Chloe, cutting off the fart mid-trump by pulling out the whoopee cushion from under her bottom again. Harry smiled, held out both his hands and received a high-five from both his dad AND mum.

'MUM?!' Chloe shrieked.

'What? Credit where credit is due, Chloe,' said Mum.

'You really did ask for that one,' added Dad, shuffling

awkwardly in his seat. 'Oh, by the way, remember that I can't take you to school today, Chloe.'

'Wait, what?!' said Chloe, jumping to her feet and instantly regretting it. She rolled back on to her heels and the pain subsided.

'I did tell you, didn't I?' said Dad, losing conviction with every syllable.

'NO! I would have left already if I knew I had to walk,' she said, brushing her hair while trying to put on her coat with the other hand.

'Yeah, I was thinking you should probably get a move on,' said Dad, taking a sip of his tea (which didn't have milk in, so he had my instant respect).

Chloe grunted in frustration, finished brushing her hair and zipped up her coat. As she bent down to pick up her school bag, Harry pressed the whoopee cushion in his hands.

TOOOOOOOOOT!

Her family laughed.

'I didn't even sit on it!' She purposefully bumped into Harry on her way to the front door, hobbling around the table to do so.

'Your brother just has perfect comedic timing,' said her dad, patting him on the back.

'I hate you all!' she screamed back as she slammed the door closed. I felt compelled to shout it too, but it came out as a BUZZZZ. At that moment I could completely understand why she hated her family so much, and I was both angry and sad.

I moved over to the back door to leave, just as Chloe's mum whipped round and walked straight towards me. She slapped me right in the face and shooed me out of the door.

'Stupid fly,' she said.

GATE'S CLOSED

It was a gorgeous, bright and sunny day.

Everywhere else.

Over Chloe (and therefore me as I caught up with her) it was raining. There was only the smallest patch of cloud in the sky but it opened up and emptied itself over Chloe. The rain soon turned into hail the size of golf balls. We took cover under a bus shelter.

I wondered what Chloe saw when she looked at me. Sometimes it's really hard to tell what people see when I'm covered in gloop, unless they acknowledge me. I had worked out that her mum had seen a fly because I'm basically a super detective (and the fact she wafted her hand at me and said 'Stupid fly' may have helped), but I wasn't sure what Chloe was seeing. She was drinking from a carton, looking through me at her own reflection in the bus shelter window, playing with her hair. She finished the drink, then threw it at me. It was not the first time I had been mistaken for a bin.

As she let go of the carton Chloe's dad pulled up in his car.

'This is spectacular, isn't it?! I've never seen anything like it!' he said from the safety of his car. 'What are you doing here? You don't need to take the bus to school,' he added.

'I was just taking shelter, you know, from the golf balls raining down on me.'

'It's ice, baby cakes, not actual golf balls, silly. Good idea.' Chloe moved towards the car. 'Whoa, I'd stay under there for a minute or two if I were you. Anyways, gotta dash or I'll be late for work!' He sped off without looking back.

'Dad!'

Chloe was furious. I desperately wanted to reach

out and put my arm around her shoulder to comfort her, but the gloop stopped that from being possible. I should explain a little further how gloop works. Chloe was seeing me as a bin, but that didn't turn me into a bin. I was still me, occupying the same space a seven-foot electric-blue alien should occupy.

However, as she perceived me to be the size and shape of a bin, if she were to touch me, she would simply feel as if she was touching a bin. Gloop plays with people's perception and it's zunking awesome! Well, mostly. When her mum slapped me, she felt a little connection on her hand as if she was wafting away a fly. I felt a belting old slap in the face. But if I put my arm around Chloe, it would terrify the life out of her. Having a bin reach out and touch you would not be comforting in the slightest!

The hail lasted for a few minutes, but with every passing second I could feel Chloe becoming more anxious about being late. She was already late before setting off, and now she was going to be super late. As soon as the hail subsided, she decided to sprint.

The only problem was, she wasn't much of a sprinter. Especially with two stubbed and still painful toes.

She tripped almost immediately, falling face first into a muddy puddle, which was absolutely freezing. Not surprising, considering it was full of ice cubes after the hailstorm, and it was much deeper than it looked. And that's when the bees came.

One after another, a swarm of bees surrounded Chloe while she lay drenched in this massive ice puddle. She was stung a couple of times on the back of her neck, and then I was very surprised to see her dive into the puddle, as if this would magic all the bees away (it didn't). She stayed under the water for about forty-five seconds before resurfacing, to see the bees waiting for her. She howled in frustration.

Pain or not in her toes, she climbed out and this time she found the strength to sprint away. I was about to follow when the bees turned on me. Here's the thing I learnt about bees. Gloop doesn't work on them. A seven-foot electric-blue alien? Who cares, get away from our house that we have been building in the corner of the bus stop, thank you very much. Or perhaps they too saw me as a bin and thought there was something sticky and sweet inside.

SIDE NOTE – I hate bees.*

They stung me EVERYWHERE. Howling with pain myself, I ran after Chloe, catching up with her just as she had managed to swat away the last of the bees.

And that's about the time the hail started up again. We both looked back longingly at the bus stop, the only shelter in a half-mile radius. But even from that distance we could see a swarm of bees hovering just above it, as if out on patrol.

Our heads down, we both rubbed our bee-stings and trudged on towards her school, as hailstone after hailstone smashed down on to us, leaving us bruised and battered. Just as we got to the school gates, the caretaker was locking them. Chloe ran over and grabbed the bars as he closed the padlock and scrambled the numbers to the code.

---

* Although I hate bees, I should point out they are one of the most important – if not THE most important – species in the Universe. Most planets have some form of bees. Considering how zunking different planets can be, that in itself is remarkable, but they always play an important role in the planet's ecosystem.
On Earth they help pollinate flowers and on Planet Lol their honey helps people laugh through some of the WORST-produced TV comedy in the entire Universe. It really is AWFUL.

'Sorry, Mr Finchley, I have had a TERRIBLE morning!'

'I can see that,' he said, looking her up and down.

'My brother, farting, a freezing puddle, bees, the hail – did you *see* the hail?! And I stubbed my toe. BOTH my toes.'

Standing next to her, I nodded in complete agreement. As much as I could see this was a terrible day (which was good for the book), I was desperate for him to open the gate for the poor girl.

He looked her up and down once again, with no sign of emotion whatsoever. Not even I could feel anything coming off him. It was super weird. 'Gate's closed,' he said.

'Yes, I can see that, but given EVERYTHING I have been through, could you PLEASE open it up for me?'

He paused, looking directly at her, before saying, 'Gate opens at three.' He turned away and walked back towards the school. It was a VERY un-Empathian thing to do and I was zunking shocked by his behaviour.

'Bloomin' marvellous!' she screamed, shaking the gate ferociously. A real pang of empathy hit me bang, smack in the stomach. It was like a stubbed toe in my stomach. A stubbed stomach. That's not really a thing, but it kinda should be, don't you think? It was a culmination of all the things that had happened in such a short time frame. Poor Chloe.

She walked the long way round to the back gate, making her way across muddy fields full of leaves that rubbed against our legs and had a real sting to them.

When she arrived at the gate, Mr Finchley was just slamming that padlock shut. It seemed he had waited for her to arrive before doing so, though his face gave absolutely no indication of smug satisfaction.

'Gate's closed,' he said, before turning away and walking off. I was fascinated by his lack of emotion, but had no time to dwell on it.

Chloe screamed. I had half a mind to rub the gloop off, pick her up and place her safely on the other side of the gate. As I contemplated breaking my no-involvement rule, Chloe looked for a way over the gate.

'Sure are a lot of bins around here,' she said, looking at me a little confused. Then she placed her foot on my head and hoisted herself up.

She navigated her way to the top of the gate fairly easily, but while swinging her leg over, she caught her skirt on a bit of loose wire and it ripped a big hole, exposing her pants.

Although no one was there to see her, I felt the sheer heat of her embarrassment burning through my cheeks. I couldn't stand by and watch any longer. This planet was full of pain and I had plenty to tell the folks back home already. *Surely I could help a little*, I thought ...

I gave her a gentle push, just as she was pulling at her skirt, trying to set it free. But I'd timed my push poorly and she fell to the ground into a thick, muddy puddle that was more mud than puddle. Basically, she fell into a pile of wet mud. I felt awful. *Oh, skonkle plop!!* That's what happens when I try to help people*, I thought. I promised myself that would be the VERY last time I got involved.

Chloe picked herself up and banged the gate in

---

* Oh, dear ... Sorry, this is not a nice term, and something I only ever use when I'm really frustrated. A skonkle plop is ... How do I put this ... Well, a skonkle is one of the largest creatures in the Universe, roughly the size of Earth's Moon. And a skonkle PLOP is what it produces after it's eaten a few too many fiery asteroids. It is, without doubt, the stinkiest and most volatile poo in the Universe.

frustration, and the padlock fell to the ground. In the distance, she heard Mr Finchley shout, 'But I left the gate unlocked.' He said this without turning round.

Chloe Harrison, sopping from head to toe, battered and bruised by hailstones the size of golf balls, covered in stings from bees and nettles, smothered in mud with a ripped skirt that had exposed her pants, finally entered school forty-five minutes late.

She tried to sneak into the back of the class, but given her appearance (and smell) this was an impossible task.

'What on earth happened to you?' asked Miss Young, with a mixed look of anger and concern on her face.

'Bees, mud, fence, whoopee cushion, hail, high-five, puddle, stupid fly, stinging nettles, more hail, stupid dad, gate closed, bins and two stubbed toes ...' said Chloe in what she seemed to think was a coherent sentence (I mean, I understood it pretty well but ...). The class laughed. The burning in my cheeks grew hotter.

Miss Young's face flipped back and forth between

anger and concern before finally settling on one.

'Oh, Chloe,' she began, guiding her to a seat at the front of the class. 'I have heard some excuses in my time but that has to be the absolute WORST! You expect me to believe you were attacked by bees? Or that you were caught in some sort of *hailstorm*? Look outside!' Miss Young pointed to the window. It was glaring sunshine.

I screamed, 'Show her your stings and bruises!' But it seemed that collectively the class had decided to see me as some sort of flying insect and only heard a buzz (apart from one kid who was looking at me and licking his lips. Pretty sure he was hungry, and saw me as some kind of sandwich …).

I could feel that the chill was now really settling in for Chloe after her icy dunkings and it took all of her energy just to sit down. Unfortunately, as she sat down the chair broke and she collapsed in a heap on the floor.

She was having such a bad morning she had moved past the point of tears. I had seen this before; in fact, it was a staple of all the worst days I had ever seen. So much happens so quickly that you don't even have time to react. The tears would inevitably flow, but always when you least expected it.

The class were laughing and pointing as she got to her feet.

'Stop messing around!' screamed Miss Young. 'Chairs don't grow on trees, you know.'

Looking at the broken wooden chair and then out of the window at some trees, I concluded quite quickly that chairs pretty much *did* grow on trees. I had only been on the planet for a day and had figured this out. It was quite concerning that an adult Earthling, tasked with teaching little Earthlings, hadn't.

The school bell rang and all the kids jumped up and ran out of the room as Miss Young continued to shout at poor Chloe, who sat silently on the floor. It was AWFUL. Finally Chloe trudged outside and burst into tears. I followed her out and did the same.

Then a boy approached her cautiously. He put a hand on her shoulder to comfort her, something I wish

I could have done. She instantly felt calmer.

'Rough day?' he said.

Chloe nodded and then burst into tears again.

'I was wondering if maybe you wanted to go and get some ice cream with me after school?' he asked.

Chloe's eyes lit up and I got a strong sense that she would very much like to do that. However, for some reason she was incapable of getting the words out. A feeling of warm embarrassment flushed her cheeks. She finally nodded, and he smiled.

'OK, I'll see you at the school gate at three p.m.' The boy walked away and for the first time that day, Chloe smiled.

I'll be honest, as much as I was searching for stories of woe to tell my fellow Empathians, I was happy to see this day take a turn for the better. Chloe was such a sweet girl and she had already been through enough. I knew the day was turning into a good day for her.

How did I know? Well, there is no such thing as a bad day that ends with ice cream. This, in my opinion, is a fact. I have seen some people have some zunking awful days. I've seen people chased by T-Rexes on their way to church. I've seen people fall down reverse waterfalls (or should I say fall up?). I have seen people get stuck in a giant's toilet, the day after that giant ate something that disagreed with them ...

BUT no matter how bad the day, ice cream ALWAYS makes things better. One small lick and suddenly everything is Zoop, Zap, Zop. It's the Universe's way of saying, 'Chin up, it'll be all right, kiddo.'

In fact, I always ensure that every alien I encounter gets an ice cream the next day. The BEST ice cream they have ever tasted, because I order it from the best ice cream parlour in the Universe: The Licktastic Original

Lollies Emporium, or LOL-E* for short.

An ice cream from LOL-E comes in every conceivable flavour. You just stick it in your mouth and it tastes like your favourite thing. For me it's a delicacy from Empathia known as Kangerine. The closest I have come to seeing it anywhere else was on Earth, where it is commonly referred to as Marmite.

I was so happy (as was Chloe) that her day was turning around that I decided I would get her the ice cream early. After all, she was going to get ice cream anyway. All I had to do was order it in and switch it with whatever they order and hey presto – BEST. ICE CREAM. EVER!

I took out my phone and dialled the number for LOL-E as I had done so many times before. It was so easy to remember because of their catchy jingle. I appreciate you won't be able to hear it when reading, but try to sing along all the same (put it to a catchy tune!).

'One, one, one … one, one … one one one, one … one, one, one. One, one, one … one, one … one one

---

* This ice cream is actually manufactured on Planet Lol using Rofel bee honey. Just a tiny bit, enough to put a smile on anyone's face!

one, one ... one, one, one.

'One, one, one ... one, one ... one one one, one ...
one, one, one.

'One, one, one ... one, one ... one one one, one ...
one, one, one.

'One, one, one ... one, one ... one one one, one ...
one, one, one.

'One, one, one ... one, one ... one one one, one ...
one, one, one.

'One, one, one ... one, one ... one one one, one ...
one, one, one.

'One.

'One.

'ONE ONE ELEVEN!!!!!!!!'

It's SO catchy.

It was ringing ...

'Hello, and thank you for dialling One, one, one ...
one—'

'Yes, I know the number very well, thank you. Not
my first time,' I said.

'Oh, excellent. I shall skip the formalities for you

then, sir. You're through to Cruncher. How can I be of service today?' he said.

'I would like to use your services, please. A nice little surprise for a life form on Planet Earth. It really is a rather breathtaking planet,' I said, smiling as I watched Chloe trip over her own feet on the way back to class. A minor setback, I thought. I'm sure things are on the turn. After all … ICE CREAM.

'Of course! Name?' asked Cruncher.

'Oh, uh, Mylan. Mylan Bletzleburger.'

'No, not your name, although it sure is an almighty pleasure to make your acquaintance, Mylan. I need the name of the life form.'

'I see. Sorry. Chloe. Chloe Harrison.'

'Of the *species*, Mr Bletzleburger. If you don't mind.'

'Earthlings, I think … I'm sorry, why do you need to know that exactly?' I had called many times before and they had never asked this question.

'It makes it much easier for us if we know who we are dealing with,' said Cruncher. I wondered if perhaps they had discovered that different life forms had different allergies and they wanted to make sure they delivered the right ice cream. A good additional check, in my opinion.

'Excellent, now we are getting somewhere. And what is the name of the planet?'

'Mylan,' I said without thinking.

'No, that's your name again, Mr Bletzleburger.'

'Sorry, long story. It's Planet Earth.'

'OK, excellent. We will be there in a jiffy. 347 jiffies, to be exact. You have an excellent day, Mr Bletzleburger, and thank you for your business this fine morning, afternoon, evening or apocalypse,' said Cruncher, before the phone went dead.

Apocalypse? Did he just say *apocalypse*? I must have misheard. Perhaps he said Calippo. A pretty popular ice lolly right across the Universe. That makes much more sense. Yes. He definitely said *Calippo*.

I followed Chloe back to the classroom, excited about the wonderful ice cream she was about to have delivered. Suddenly something pressed itself against the window. It was small, green and at first looked like a leaf. It was joined by another, then another and before long the small green things had the full attention of the class.

'Miss Young, what is ...' But Chloe trailed off, her eyes fixated on the window, which was almost entirely covered with ...

'Business cards?' said Miss Young, as if trying to convince herself. 'They look like business cards ...' She stood up and went over to the window. She opened it, and hundreds of cards flew into the room.

I thought this was a typical Earth school event, but from the confusion I could feel coming from everyone, it seemed it wasn't normal.

We could hear a similar rumble of confusion coming from the other classrooms. Miss Young went to the corridor, closely followed by her class. She looked up. More of the strange cards were covering the skylight that ran the length of the corridor.

'What on earth ...' said Mr Myers, the head teacher, who had wandered out of his office and was looking around in bemusement.

---

* This means crazy, named after an alien creature that spends its life spinning in circles. The Floo Floo spins, falls down, gets back up again, then continues spinning over and over again.
On its birthday, as a treat, it will spin the other way for the day. No one can figure out quite why they do it and when asked they simply say, 'Ask me again when I'm not so dizzy.'
They are pretty crazy.

'They're everywhere!' said one of the other teachers who had emerged from another class.

I wasn't surprised to see that the Earthlings had no idea what was going on; they seemed pretty clueless to me. But the fact I didn't know either was making me go a little floo floo.*

I stared at the card in the same wide-eyed bewilderment as the Earthlings around me.

The 'Universal Life Form Recycling Agency'. I had never heard of them, but it seems they were on their way to recycle Earth. More importantly, it turned out that Chloe's day wasn't getting any better after all.

'Oh, skonkle plop!' I said.

Thank you for using the **UNIVERSAL LIFEFORM RECYCLING AGENCY**. This planet is being recycled.

You're welcome.

If you have any issues with our service (which is highly doubtful as you have most likely been recycled), please call us on:

11111111111111 11111111111111 11111111111111
11111111111111 11111111111111 11111111111111

ELEVEN

Or, preferably, don't.

ULRA

DID YOU SAY CALIPPO?

I stared at the number on the card, going through the jingle in my head. I had dialled an extra 1! I hadn't called for ice cream at all! I felt zunking AWFUL. The worst I have ever felt. I have got involved in people's bad days before and made them worse, but never had I accidentally recycled their entire planet along with everyone living on it. Pushing Chloe into mud was nothing compared to this.

I hastily dialled the number on the card.

'Hello and thank you for dialling one—'

'I don't have time for this. Please, I need your help!' I said frantically.

'Why, of course, sir, I have just the thing. How about a Calippo?'

'That's the problem, the apocalypse is already— Wait, did you say *Calippo*?'

'One of the finest ice creams in the Universe, served daily by us lolly-loving folk at LOL-E. Using just a hint of Rofel bee honey—'

'ARGH!' I screamed, and hung up. I dialled again – counting the ones methodically – and managed to get through to ULRA this time.

'Good morning, afternoon, evening or apocalypse—'

'Yes, yes, enough of that. I don't have time,' I said impatiently.

'Must be the apocalypse. What can I do for you today? You're speaking to Cruncher.'

'Brilliant! Cruncher, it's me, Mylan Bletzleburger. We spoke a few moments ago,' I said, happy that I had managed to get the exact same call-centre specialist, at what must have been astronomical odds.

'Sorry, sir, we haven't spoken before. We are all called Cruncher here. Makes us sound more menacing, you know?' said Cruncher very politely. 'We are actually a call-centre planet with the highest customer satisfaction rating in the Universe, due to our calm nature and extreme politeness.'

'I don't give a skonkle plop about that,' I said impatiently. 'I'd like to make a complaint.'

'Well now, I am VERY sorry to hear that, but please, sir, I must ask you to mind your language.'

'Oh ... sorry,' I said, and I meant it, because I'd used that horrible term again (apologies to you too, dear reader!).

'No problem, Mr Bletzleburger. Now, to your predicament, it really breaks my heart. If I'm honest, I'm completely devastated and I will do absolutely everything I can to help. Let me just take a few important details from you,' said Cruncher in an annoyingly cheery manner. 'Firstly, let me ask how is your day going.'

'Terrible! Because—'

'Terrible. OK, fantastic. I've popped that down for you. Now, let me ask, have you recently discovered your planet is due to be recycled?'

'No—'

'Oh, good. We can avoid a very difficult discussion then,' said Cruncher.

'It's not my planet. I just happen to be on it. I accidentally dialled the wrong number. I was trying to get hold of an ice cream company.'

'LOL-E?' asked Cruncher.

'YES! You've heard of it?'

'Only the best ice cream in the Universe! I love a Calippo, I really do.'

'Perfect! The numbers are incredibly similar; it really is an easy mistake to make.'

'Well, they are very different. We have an extra 1 and they have a VERY catchy jingle. But don't worry, sir, I'd be happy to help,' said Cruncher kindly.

I felt a huge sense of relief, as I watched everyone panic around me. Some kids were running around laughing, thinking it was a prank. Some kids were sobbing in groups. The teachers were watching the news on their phones. The cards had been found all over the little blue and green planet, it seemed. It would take some effort to clear them all up, but at least I was about to save Earth.

'Thank you. What do you need me to do?' I asked.

'Not a problem. It's quite simple really. Step one, get off the planet.'

'OK ...' I said reluctantly, not sure how that was going to help the situation. I waited patiently to hear more, but Cruncher said nothing. 'And step two?' I asked.

'Not needed. You'll be happy to hear that this is a one-step programme. Get off the planet as it's being recycled. I assume you have a spaceship?'

'Yes, but—'

'Then I would get in said spaceship and leave the planet within ... the next two minutes.'

'But I was just trying to order ice cream!' I said in desperation.

'The ULRA doesn't currently offer ice-cream-related services. We deal solely in the recycling of planets. However, you can get hold of the Universe's best ice cream company by dialling one, one, one—' Cruncher began to cheerily sing the theme tune.

'I know the number!' I screamed.

'I think given your current situation, that isn't strictly true …'

'So I can't stop the planet being recycled?'

'I'm afraid not, but what I will say is I wish you a FANTASTIC apocalypse,' said Cruncher with far too much good cheer.

'It's NOT the apocalypse!'

'It soon will be, unless you follow our one-step programme. Have a good morning, afternoon, evening or in your case—'

I hung up the phone and rushed outside.

Everywhere I looked, all I could see were the ULRA business cards. They had stopped falling from the sky, but they seemed to cover every inch of the planet. I couldn't see a single blade of grass in the playing field. The printing costs must have been astronomical.

I let the collective fear of the planet wash over me for a few seconds and it was unlike any fear I had ever felt. They were absolutely terrified. I focused back in on Chloe, who was a mixture of scared and confused. I stood right next to her as she stared at the cards by her feet.

I called my spaceship with a click of my fingers (I know, I know. It's pretty dated technology, but what can I say? No Vansarian Tech here; I'm old school).

Within seconds it was hovering next to me in the playground. I took it off incognito mode. After all, the entire planet had just been told it was going to be recycled; there was no sense trying not to scare the Earthlings any more. Aliens exist. They needed to get over it pretty quickly.

'Is that a spaceship?!' screamed Miss Young (who had clearly not got over it), but she was pointing into the sky overhead, rather than at my ship.

I looked up to see a gargantuan ship hovering above the entire world. A ship bigger than the planet itself and it was jet black (the coolest ships are *always* jet black). It had blocked out the sun, but it had spotlights trained on us so that we could see each other. And admire the ship, I guess? It was very cool.

'Hello ... Ear ... E-yar ... Urt ... How do you say this?' said a booming voice, which was coming directly from the ship. The sound quality was incredible. The ship had hyper-placement speakers that played sound at the perfect pitch and distance from your ears to ensure the optimum listening experience. It was pretty fancy stuff that I couldn't help but admire (as I said, I'm a bit of a spaceship nerd).

All the Earthlings put their hands over their ears as if it was somehow hurting them (it wasn't. Like I said, it was *perfect*) but was probably more them being in shock.

'Earth? ... Really? ... Are you sure, Glob?' The voice seemed to be having a discussion with another alien. 'They named their entire planet after the ground they walk on? But look at it. It's mostly water! Why name it after the land?! ... HA! HA! HA! ... Sorry, what? ... I'm fully aware we aren't the best life form at naming things either. Why do you have to be such a skonkle plop, Glob? ... Ah yes, sorry. As I was saying, hello, EAR-TH. As you know, your planet and all creatures within it are about to be recycled ...'

The message was blaring out across the planet in all known languages and the collective response from Earth was so loud it could be heard by the ship above. It was a huge scream followed by a lengthy bout of sobbing.

'Don't scream at me, I'm just doing my job!' boomed the voice. It sounded a little offended. 'If you want to be annoyed with someone, then aim your screams at ...' He paused again and I could hear him flicking through some papers. I knew exactly what he was going to say and although no one had any idea who I was, I didn't plan to stick around.

'... Mylan Bletzleburger! That's who you should be angry with. He was the one who marked you for recycling. Wait, what?' said the captain, clearly talking to Glob again. 'Not again! That has to be the third time this week! When will people learn? People of EAR-TH, listen to this, it will really give you a good chuckle. This Mylan Bletzleburger character, apparently he was trying to order ice cream and he called us instead! Isn't that HILARIOUS?! Oh, well ... Good morning, afternoon or in your case apocalypse to you all!'

The captain turned off his microphone and the world fell into silence once more. Then a few extraordinary things happened in quick succession.

Every single human exclaimed at the exact same

time, 'Who on earth is Mylan Bletzleburger?!'

Then a planetary stasis gun fired at Earth, freezing every living creature on the planet.

And finally, the front of the gargantuan spaceship opened up and began to swallow Planet Earth whole.

THERE'S MORE?!

'So this planet got swallowed *whole* by a spaceship?!
How big was the planet? No, wait, how big was the
SPACESHIP!' said Flobble, clearly very excited.

'The planet was about three times the size of K'POW,'
I replied. I had expected this revelation to be greeted by
a significant amount of head wobbling and I was not
disappointed.

'I can't even begin to think of ... The sheer size of
the ship needed ...' said Flobble in awe. 'Maybe it uses
some sort of Vansarian Tech?'

'Unlikely,' said Heather plainly. 'You wouldn't believe
the things I had to do to get hold of this hairdryer,'

she said, staring into space. No one dared ask her any questions.

'And you're telling me the very last thing those people thought about before being frozen in time was, "Who is Mylan Bletzleburger?"!' said Blurgh. I nodded solemnly and Blurgh burst with laughter (this is quite common for the inhabitants of K'POW, who find it pretty easy to reassemble their gelatinous bodies after bursting).

'Ignore him,' said Flobble, offering a stern look that Blurgh didn't notice as he pulled himself together. 'I assume that you weren't on Earth when the freeze gun hit?'

'No, I was not. I managed to get on to my ship and out of the planet's atmosphere just in time.'

'So ... is that the end? Chloe and her entire planet get recycled. That seems like the worst day ever to me!' said Flobble.

'No ...' I said.

'There's MORE?!' said Blurgh.

'Unfortunately,' I said with a sigh. 'Because as I

watched Planet Earth get swallowed up, I discovered something that was zunking floo floo.'

'What?!' said Flobble.

'That I wasn't the only one to escape on my ship.'

OLD FAITHFUL

I had been covered in gloop for the best part of six hours by then and it was starting to stink. It was super sticky too. After two or three hours it also really begins to irritate my skin, so I got out my best towels and a bowl of cool scented water to scrub it off as I watched the gargantuan spaceship swallow Planet Earth.

It is honestly one of the strangest things I have ever seen. I was watching from a respectable distance (if you know the area, I was by a place called the Moon) and it was a bit like watching a space snake eat an asteroid. It didn't look like it should be possible, but little by little, the planet was being swallowed up.

I sat scrubbing my face, watching in silence, thinking about what I had done. I obviously felt a tremendous amount of guilt. I couldn't help but blame myself. Mostly because it was my fault. The worst part though? I could feel Chloe's pain.

Although she was frozen and on Earth, her pain was so strong I could still feel it. It can't be easy knowing your planet is about to be recycled, all because some weird alien doesn't know how to order ice cream.

It felt like she was having some sort of out-of-body experience. Like she wasn't on the doomed planet, frozen with all her family and friends, but instead was hovering high above, watching it all unfold. I could feel her sorrow and horror from the other side of the Moon. And then there was a spark of anger. Pure, blood-boiling anger. The sort of anger you feel when you've had the worst day ever and then your planet gets swallowed by a giant spaceship. There was so much pent-up anger, it felt like she simply had to lash out at the closest possible person immediately or she would burst!

'OUCH!' I screamed. It felt like I had been hit on the head with a shoe. It was a strange feeling, as it felt like Chloe was attacking someone with a shoe, and as well as feeling her anger, I was feeling the pain of the victim too.

'OUCH!!!!' I screamed louder the second time as another shoe struck the back of my head. I turned round just in time to see a schoolbook come flying towards my face.

'WHO ARE YOU? NO, WAIT, *WHAT* ARE YOU, AND WHAT IS HAPPENING TO MY PLANET?!' screamed Chloe.

I looked at her, then back out of my window a few times, trying to understand what was going on. After a few moments and a couple more screams, it was as clear as day. Chloe was on my ship, and she was cross. ZUNKING cross. So cross that the fact she was on a spaceship with an alien didn't bother her at all.

'I don't understand. How did you ...' I mumbled.

'YOU don't understand?! I've just watched my entire planet get swallowed up by a spaceship, having been abducted by some weird blue … thingy. And before today I didn't even think aliens existed!' said Chloe. She'd made a couple of very valid points.

Firstly, I had rubbed off my gloop, so she was seeing me in all my electric-blue glory (however she still threw stuff at me like I was a bin, so not a lot had changed on that front). Secondly, she thought she had been abducted.

'Wait, sorry … Abducted? I did NOT abduct you,' I said defiantly, stupidly thinking this was the most important thing to discuss.

'Well, I didn't abduct myself, did I?' said Chloe, planting her feet firmly on the ground and offering out her hands as if she was handcuffed. It was a little overdramatic, but another valid point all the same.

'Yeah, well … I guess not.' Then it hit me. I may not have abducted her, but my SHIP might have. 'Ah … I didn't abduct you, but *Old Faithful* might have.'

'Who is "Old Faithful"?' asked Chloe, quickly snapping her head round to check for anyone else behind her.

'My ship. She is programmed to help me or anyone I am with if they are in grave danger. She must have sensed the planet was about to be recycled and whiiiiiiiiiiisshhhhoooooooop –' I made the sound *Old Faithful* makes when beaming someone on board – 'here you are.'

'With you? I wasn't *with you*.'

'No …' I said, unsure of how to explain. 'But she might have thought *I* was with *you*. Silly old ship!' I said, playfully punching the dashboard as if this explained everything.

Chloe picked up her shoe and hit me with it in response.

'What is happening to my planet?' she repeated, heading over to the window, desperate for a glimpse. She was scratching her head and pacing the floor, clearly agitated.

'Um … I think it's being recycled,' I said cautiously.

'Recycled?! I think you mean DESTROYED!' This time she went out of her way to hit me. She packed an almighty punch for someone so small. She then pushed

past me and headed back to the window. 'Wait … It's
… gone!' She pressed her face against the window and
breathed heavily, fogging up the glass.

I came over and rubbed away the fog so I could see.
Planet Earth had disappeared and all I could see was
the giant spaceship.

'I … Look, I feel we've got off on the wrong shoe
– I mean FOOT – here, Chloe. My name is Mylan
Bletzleburger …'

'How do you know my name?' she said, pushing
herself away from the glass and facing me. Then a
harrowed look of recognition flashed across her face.
'Mylan Bletzlebunny …'

'Burger. Bletzle*burger*,' I said.

'That's the name the aliens gave … The *other* aliens.'
She stomped her foot like a bull getting ready to
charge.

'Now, hold on …' I said, desperately trying to think of
one good reason she should hold on before laying into
me or, worse, charging at me. My mind was blank.

'They said if you want someone to blame, speak to

Mylan Bletzlebooger.'

'Not exactly,' I said, which was strictly true as my name isn't Bletzle*booger*.

'YOU did this! To MY planet! All my friends, family ... All those people ... WHY?!' Her cheeks grew redder as her breathing got heavier.

'I didn't mean— It was never my— I was just trying to order some ice cream for you!' I cried hopelessly.

I thought she was about to throw another of what seemed to be an endless supply of shoes, as the anger bubbled inside her to boiling point. She stomped her feet a few more times and let out a grunt of frustration before charging towards me. I closed my eyes and braced for impact. It didn't come. I opened my eyes, but Chloe wasn't there. That's when I heard two BLEEPS, a BLOOP and a BLOP coming from *Old Faithful*'s dashboard. I turned to find Chloe desperately mashing away at ALL the buttons.

'Hey! Don't do that!' I said, rushing over to stop her.

Chloe snarled at me and picked up her button-mashing pace. 'One of these buttons MUST release my planet,' she said. Having hit every button on the dashboard, she now did it again, only harder.

I reached out to grab her arm, but was hit in the face by a jet of water. Chloe had activated the fire extinguisher. I covered my eyes and tried to pull her away, but she had managed to order a pizza, which flew through the air and hit me in the face. That was one of my personal designs – the pizza was cooked as it flew through the air ready for me to catch it on a plate. It looked pretty cool and delicious, but this time the plate had been my face.

'COME ON!' she screamed in frustration, trying out different combinations of buttons, all the while looking out into the vast empty space where Earth had once been. In the thirty seconds she was in control she had managed to: enable party mode, blasting music and disco lights on the deck; activate zero-gravity mode (she barely noticed, her legs lifting behind her as she continued to hammer the controls, eventually turning it off); and, most annoyingly, reset ALL the clocks on the ship including the one on the microwave, which was an absolute NIGHTMARE to set to the correct time.

A final BLEEP, BLOOP, BLOP later and *Old Faithful* said, 'Are you sure you would like to activate rewind mode?' Chloe's eyes lit up. I shook my head dramatically, causing the pizza to finally fall off my face, but it was too late.

'YES!' she screamed, hammering down on the control panel.

Everything that had happened on the deck in the past two minutes whizzed by in reverse. The pizza flew back to the dashboard, the water flowed back into the fire extinguisher, Chloe retracted her punch from me, and paced back and forth from the window, and the shoes and schoolbook flew from my head back to Chloe's hand.

As the reversal stopped, Chloe collapsed in a heap on the floor, utterly exhausted. I was not far behind.

'What the—' she managed, as she lay next to me looking up at the ceiling.

'It's a localised reversal,' I gasped. 'It doesn't actually turn back time, nor does it affect anything outside the ship. It's really just there in case you drop a glass or something.'

'Oh ... Or if you stub your toe maybe,' she said, thinking back on her morning.

'Precisely,' I said, sitting up.

Chloe joined me and looked me over quizzically as

if she was trying to figure out a riddle. 'So my planet …'
She managed to pull herself up using the dashboard to
look out of the window.

'Still gone, I'm afraid,' I said.

'I just don't understand,' she managed to mutter
breathlessly.

'I … uh … It's a long story,' I said cautiously.

'I have all the time in the world,' she said, realising
instantly that her world now had NO time. Finally her
steely exterior and fearsome guard dropped and she
burst into tears. Being an Empathian, I joined in too.

We cried side by side for almost twenty minutes. It
was exhausting. When we finally stopped, I told her
my story. How I grew up on Empathia; how my parents
visited Earth (but thought it was called Mylan – she
managed a polite chuckle at their mistake); how I
visited planets across the Universe, only to discover
how many people were in pain; how my parents had
lied; how I was desperate to help so I started writing
a book; how she had become the latest chapter; how
I had felt her stub her toe, that her mum had slapped

me and how she had thought I was a bin; that I was just trying to order her and that boy some ice cream.

'I'm sorry,' I said, feeling completely and emotionally drained. 'I was just trying to help.'

She remained mostly silent throughout my story, but my apology reduced her to tears once more. Before the uncontrollable sobbing took me over again too, I got the slightest sense of what was upsetting her. Had I been some vile monster, with TERRIBLE hair, it would have been easy to keep the anger building. To fight me no matter how pointless it might be. But to hear me apologise and to see that I was trying to make the Universe a better place was almost worse. She simply hadn't expected the destroyer of her world to be so ... nice.

After quite some time of harmonised sobbing, Chloe jumped to her feet.

'OK. OK, this is good,' she said, clapping her hands. I looked at her, puzzled. 'OK, not Earth and everyone on it being destroyed because you don't know how to order ice cream, or the fact your parents lied to your entire planet, or that we are both desperate to return home but neither of us can ... Wait, what was I saying?'

'That this is good. I think?' I wasn't sure. None of it sounded at all good to me.

'Ah yes, good! What's good is that I am in the company of an alien who is desperate to help people in this Universe, right?' she said, nodding her head at me eagerly.

'Yes ...' I said cautiously, returning a gentle nod.

'Then there is still hope!' she said. 'You want to help. I need help, because my planet is being destroyed. That is a match made in heaven if you ask me.'

'Sure,' I said, trying to think about how we could save an entire planet. 'Help, *how*? I'm not exactly sure *how* we can ... It's just such a big spaceship ... and there are only two of us ...' I trailed off. The cogs began to turn in my brain (this is another Earth expression. I don't have actual cogs in my brain, unlike cyborgs). 'I guess if we could get on board that spaceship ...' I began.

'Yes ...' said Chloe.

'And we could bypass their security systems ...'

'Yes ...' She leaned in closer.

'And we could discover some kind of weakness ...'

'Yes ...'

'Then your planet would still be doomed. I'm sorry, Chloe. I have absolutely no idea what I'm talking about.'

Chloe folded her arms and frowned at me. It didn't take being an Empathian to realise she was not happy with my answer. 'But you HAVE to help me; it's part of who you are!' She slammed her hand on the dashboard defiantly and a pizza flew across the ship and hit me in the face. Her smile indicated this was NOT by accident.

She was right. Despite flinging TWO pizzas at me, I did feel compelled to help her, but I just couldn't think of anything. Maybe ice cream? But I wasn't feeling brave enough to order that again, nor brave enough to mention it to Chloe!

I began to think about the countless alien life forms I had met during my travels and all the nuggets of knowledge they had given me. Then a spark fired up in my brain. A teeny, tiny spark, but so much can come from a little spark (just ask the good people of Zorgan

7, the Universe's only planet made entirely of fireworks. Well, at least it used to be, until a little spark …).

'What would you do if your cat ate something it shouldn't?' I said.

Chloe looked confused but gave an answer all the same. 'My cat wouldn't eat anything it shouldn't.'

'Why?'

'Curiosity killed the cat, even she knows that.'

'Oh. Poor cat. I'm so sorry for your loss,' I said.

'It's just a saying. My cat isn't … Never mind. I guess if my cat was stupid enough to eat something that she shouldn't, I would help her sick it up.'

'Exactly!' I said, as if I had laid out a fully thought-through, step-by-step plan to save the planet. Chloe obviously couldn't see it. 'That's what we need the ship to do – sick up Earth!'

'OK … but the ship isn't alive,' she said, not with one hundred per cent confidence. After all, it had been a pretty strange day so far and I talked about *Old Faithful* as if *she* was alive.

I waved my arms excitedly. 'Neither are cyborgs,

but I've seen plenty of them throw up. Bolts and oil everywhere. We just need to find something that disagrees with it and it'll come straight back up.'

'I did *not* think I would be saying this when I woke up this morning but ... what exactly makes a ship vomit up a planet?'

That was a great question. Unfortunately, before I could think about how we could get an answer, I heard bleeping coming from *Old Faithful*'s dashboard monitor.

THE SPACESHIP

At first, I simply ignored the bleeping. Probably just a bit of passing space debris. *Old Faithful* always got excited about passing space debris, like a dog yapping at the window every time a car goes past; it happened all the time. However, the bleeps didn't stop. Instead, they became more regular and close together.

'Why is it bleeping?' asked Chloe, ducking slightly as if she expected a pizza to fly towards her.

'It can only mean one thing. A ship is approaching,' I said. I ran over to the window to see a small spaceship getting bigger as it got closer. The speakers on my ship crackled, causing Chloe to cover her ears.

'What's *that* noise?!' she asked.

'That would be someone hacking into *Old Faithful*'s audio system. Poor thing, try and fight it, girl!' But it was no use, they already had access.

'This is the captain of *The Spaceship*, do you read me?' said a rather stern voice over the PA system.

I must admit I was confused, as last time I checked I was the captain of my spaceship. Not as confused as Chloe was though, as she clamped her hands tightly over her ears.

'What was that AWFUL sound?!' she said through gritted teeth.

I listened carefully but all I could hear was the faint hum of *Old Faithful*'s engine. Then I realised what she meant. She was hearing an alien language. Some of them can be pretty deafening. If you hear a Kazaam speak even one simple word without the proper equipment, your head is very likely to explode.

'It's the aliens on that other ship talking. Wait a second,' I said, running to the back room, where I began to rummage around in a couple of very full drawers that I had been meaning to clear out for the last 456 years.

'Well, it sounded awful. How come I can understand *you*?' said Chloe thoughtfully, just as I found what I was looking for.

'Because of this little beauty!' I said, holding a small electronic pill aloft. 'I need you to swallow it.' It looked like a regular pill, only it was see-through and you could see mini cogs turning and whirring.

'What is it?' she asked, taking it in her hand and inspecting it under the light.

'It's a TALK,' I said. 'It will help you communicate with other aliens and stop any unnecessary head explosions.'

Chloe looked even more confused but shrugged her shoulders and swallowed the pill. I was impressed. She had already reached the stage of intergalactic travel where nothing surprises you. This normally takes a good few years. She was adapting well.

The speakers crackled again. 'Helloooooooo, little spaceship. This is the captain of *The Spaceship*, do you read me?!' Chloe nodded and put her thumbs up.

'Um … I'm the captain of the spaceship,' I replied tentatively.

'No, you're not. I am,' the voice repeated firmly.

'Well, I'm sitting in the captain's chair so …' I said, sitting down to confirm my position.

'Wait, am I talking to someone on *The Spaceship* or the little spacecraft?' He paused, and I could hear someone murmuring to him in the background. I looked out of the window and could just about make out two aliens in the cockpit of the other spaceship. They were turned towards each other. 'I see … That's why I said we shouldn't call our spaceship *The Spaceship*. It only causes confusion, Glob.'

'So you're the captain of that zunking BIG spaceship over there? The Zoop, Zap, Zop, jet-black one that just swallowed an entire planet?' I asked, waving my hand behind me, signalling to Chloe to duck down. If I could see them, they could see us. She did, but not before shooting me a fearsome look. She didn't like me praising the ship that had swallowed her planet, which was fair enough (but it was zunking awesome ...).

'I am,' said the captain proudly.

'And it's seriously called *The Spaceship*?!' I said, trying not to laugh.

'That's what happens when you let the general public vote for a name. They think they are SO funny, but they don't think about the confusion it brings,' said the captain with more than a little annoyance.

'What can I do for you, captain of *The Spaceship*?' I asked.

'We are in the process of recycling Planet E-Art. No, that's not it. I've forgotten again. Planet ... Ear ... The blue and green planet. You saw it, right? Anyway, we believe that one of the inhabitants escaped just before the planet was put into stasis.'

'Oh, dear,' I said, frantically waving behind me to ensure Chloe remained hidden.

'Yes. Oh, dear indeed. We like to do a thorough job here at ULRA, and when we recycle a planet, that involves the entire planet and everything on it.'

'I see.' That confirmed it. They were here for Chloe. I

couldn't let them take her. I could lie to them, but that would only hold them off for so long. I needed a plan, and I needed it quickly.

'Our computers identified a spaceship—'

'Wait, do you mean *The Spaceship*?' I knew exactly what he had meant, but I was stalling for time.

'NO! Honestly, as soon as we get back I am putting in a request to change the name. Write that down, Glob. "Change the name of the ship." Underline it too.'

'Underlined, sir,' I heard Glob reply faintly in the background.

'Now, listen carefully. I meant *your* spacecraft was seen leaving, and we traced your movements back here.'

'OK ...'

'We believe that there is a huge man on your ship. Wait, that's NOT what they are called. Sorry, a *human* on your spaceship.'

'Sorry, on *The Spaceship*? I'm so confused!' I said with a smile. The captain was really easy to wind up.

'NOT *THE SPACESHIP*! That's it, as soon as we get

back we are changing the name. I'll hang off the side with a bucket of paint myself if I have to.'

'What about something simple, like *Ship*?' I said. It was the perfect suggestion as it launched the captain into a five-minute tirade about the stupidity of naming a ship *Ship*. I muted my microphone, ducked down and found Chloe.

She rolled her eyes. 'I thought aliens were meant to be smart. I mean, you travel billions of miles across the Universe, have spaceships that can swallow entire planets, yet you name spaceships *Spaceship*. It's a bit embarrassing.'

'You're right, but we don't have time to discuss that. Listen, they are after you and they aren't going to stop until they find you,' I said, going into the back room.

'Just tell them they've made a mistake. That I'm not here.'

'It won't work. They're not stupid.'

'They have a spaceship called *The Spaceship*.'

'OK, maybe they are stupid, but they won't just take my word for it, they will want proof. They'll force their way on to the ship and—' That was it. I had a plan, but there was no time to explain as I could hear the captain coming to the end of his tirade. 'I know what to do.'

'Great. What's the plan?' asked Chloe, but I didn't answer. Instead, I picked up a jar off the shelf and made my way back to the cockpit.

'… Wet blanket. Honestly, even that would be a better name for a ship! Now, do you have the human or not?' said the captain, who sounded absolutely exhausted.

'No,' I said bluntly, unscrewing the top of the jar.

'You know we can detect TWO life forms on your space … vehicle,' said the captain, seemingly unable to utter the word 'spaceship' any more.

'Yes, but the other one's not a human,' I said, looking at Chloe the human.

'Prepare to be boarded,' said the captain, who had finally run out of patience. His ship was right next to mine now.

Chloe looked at me with wide-eyed panic. I stood up, took a deep breath and said 'sorry' before launching an entire jar of gloop at her. She gasped and glared at me furiously.

Here's the thing about gloop, a little goes a long way. But when you're in a hurry, and you need to ensure an instant and long-lasting effect, it's best to use a jarful.

'What the—' Chloe was frozen to the spot, covered head to toe in gloop. 'This STINKS! Is this that gloop stuff that you put on to make you look like a bin?' she said, holding her nose.

'Yep,' I said, making sure it was fully covering her.

'What do you see?' she asked.

'What I always see.'

There was no time to explain. There was a loud crack and a puff of smoke and the captain appeared in my cockpit. He was accompanied by an alien that was perfectly round and green, resembling an oversized pea. Glob, I assumed.

The captain was short and stocky, only just taller than Glob, but he stood up so straight he seemed to tower over everyone. He had short black hair and a bulbous nose that had at least eight nostrils.

I tuned in to the captain's emotions. He was feeling incredibly anxious about finding the human and would stop at nothing to get them back. Glob was equally agitated, because he knew how irritable the captain could be when he didn't get his way.

Their anxiety made me nervous, and when I get nervous I sweat …

'Right, let's take a look at them, Glob,' said the captain, looking everywhere but right at me. Glob, who had no arms or legs, rolled towards us. As they approached, my salty sweat sprayed out of my armpits in all directions. Chloe managed to duck, but I caught Glob and the captain right in the face. They spluttered. I held my arms tight to my sides to stop any further eruptions.

'Hello, captain, I'm Mylan Bletzleburger. Sorry about that. It's a little hot in here, don't you think?' I said, offering a hand awkwardly without lifting my arm. It was duly ignored (not surprisingly from Glob, who would have had a tough time shaking anyone's hand for obvious reasons).

The captain took out a tissue and dabbed his forehead. 'Bletzleburger? You're the one who called this whole thing in, right? What was it, didn't like the look of them? One of them call you a nasty name?'

'Sweat Man, perhaps?' said Glob as he tried to dry himself by blowing upwards with his lips.

'That would certainly fit. Whatever the reason, you wanted to get rid of their entire stinking planet. I don't mind, we've heard it all,' said the captain with a smile.

'He was trying to order ice cream, remember, sir?' said Glob.

'Oh, yes! Awful mistake. TERRIBLE!' The captain slapped his knee and let out a humungous cackle. 'It has really put me in the mood for ice cream though. You must give me the number of a good place. On second thoughts, DON'T!'

I have travelled the Universe for nearly two thousand years and in that time I have never met a creature that had as little empathy as the captain (and I once visited a planet full of rocks that had the emotional intelligence of, well, rocks. They were as hard as stone, but even they showed emotion, albeit once a year when old rocks were skimmed across the great lake at the heart of the planet, never to be seen again. It really was moving. I cried for three whole days afterwards).

The captain didn't care about Earth, or any of the other planets he had encountered. He simply didn't care about anyone but himself, and for this reason alone I felt truly sorry for him.

'Come on, it might have been an accident, but there must have been *something* you didn't like about Earth?' he said, trying to push me.

'Um ... well, I didn't really like their tea,' I said. The captain looked back blankly at me. 'It's a drink. They put excreted animal liquid in it.'

'URGH, that's disgusting! You did the right thing, even if you didn't mean to!' said the captain. 'Now, if you could introduce us to whoever is on your ship with you so we can check they aren't one of those humans, we will be on our way.'

'Uh ... sure,' I said, pointing behind them at Chloe. I held my arms even tighter to my body as my nervousness increased. The problem is, you never know what or who someone is going to see. I was worried that they wanted to find a human, and therefore that is what they would see. I would have no idea what they saw, and would just have to figure it out.

'It's … YOU!' said the captain in awe, dropping to his knees. Glob panicked and rolled on to his face. This reaction was unexpected to me. Even more so for Chloe.

'Yes. It's me,' said Chloe, not sure what to do. She looked at me for help, but I simply shrugged my shoulders. She decided to fling her arms into the air dramatically and do an impromptu spin. Amazingly, her audience seemed impressed.

'But why are you travelling on a ship like this, with an alien who can't even order ice cream?' asked the captain cautiously.

'You know, I *can* actually order ice cream and have done so many times before. You accidentally recycle a planet ONE time and you never hear the end of it,' I said, instantly regretting it. Chloe shot an angry stare at me and stomped her foot.

I looked at the captain, and for the first time I could see he felt the slightest pang of empathy. He felt sorry for *me*. I tried to think who I could possibly be travelling with that would make the captain feel even the teeniest amount of empathy for me. Then an idea struck me, but if I was wrong it would ruin everything. I decided to take a leap of faith …

'I think you'll find that Her Royal Highness, Queen of the Universe, Tanka Tanka Woo Woo, can travel with whoever she deems worthy,' I said, taking an almighty guess.

'Oh, of course! I meant no offence, Your Majesty,' said the captain, grovelling.

Bingo, I was right. They were seeing the Queen of the Universe. I wish I could have seen her in the flesh too. It's my absolute DREAM to meet her one day, if only to get a close-up look of her Zoop, Zap, Zop hair.

'*Royal Highness*,' said Chloe bluntly, standing a little taller, putting on a weird accent that I can only assume she felt was befitting of royalty, but sounded more like she had a plum in her mouth. 'I'll have you address me by my proper title or not at all, captain.'

Chloe began circling the captain and Glob, demanding their attention. They naturally spun round as she moved. The captain bowed his head as he did so and muttered an apology.

I pointed at the captain and then back at his ship, mouthing the words 'get them out' at Chloe. She nodded in agreement, but I could tell she was really enjoying her new role.

'Please, we didn't know ... I'm so sorry, Your ... Royal Highness,' said the captain timidly.

She stopped suddenly and faced away from them. 'Your apology is acknowledged,' she said, before turning to face them dramatically, 'but NOT accepted.' She pointed to the ground and clicked her fingers, and the captain bowed in front of her. Chloe let out a little giggle before stomping her foot, causing them to both jump.

'Now, I must insist that you leave my ship at once,' she said firmly.

'Oh, yes, right away,' said the captain, leaping to his feet. He had to kick Glob to get him moving as he was still face down on the floor. They were just about to teleport when I saw a little spark in Chloe's eyes. The kind of spark that could blow up an entire planet (made of fireworks). I shook my head at her in a 'don't even think about it' gesture, but it seemed that Chloe had taken to her new role of Queen of the Universe a little too well.

'Oh, captain,' said Chloe, waving her hand regally and sticking her nose in the air in the opposite direction. She looked a bit like a snobby teapot.

'Yes, Your Royal Highness.'

'There is one thing you can do for me. If you do it, I may even consider accepting your apology.'

'Anything, just name it!' said the captain, clearly relieved. I could tell he did not want to travel the Universe with an unaccepted apology from Tanka Tanka Woo Woo.

'Put that little blue and green planet you just swallowed up back where you found it. There's a good boy,' she added, as an afterthought tapping him (not gently, I might add) on his head.

'Uh ...' The captain hesitated.

'Captain, your Queen is giving you an order!' Chloe clapped her hands twice abruptly. 'Chop, chop!'

'I ... yes ... but ...'

'Do you really want to make me angry? Do you have any idea what happens when I get angry?!' She was taking this too far now and with hand signals and strained eyes I pleaded with her to quit, but she simply ignored me.

'I can't,' said the captain. 'I don't have the authority. My superiors at ULRA are the only ones who can authorise a planet to be released. Even if I wanted to, I couldn't override the programming on the ship to let the planet go.'

'Then we shall call them right now!' she said, her real anger coming through. Her home planet *was* trapped in *The Spaceship*.

'It's too late. The planet-recycling program has already begun inside *The Spaceship*. It takes just twenty-four hours –' the captain looked at his watch – 'which means Earth has exactly twenty-two hours before it will be smooshed into a new planet full of clones. There is no way they would be able to sign off its release before then. The paperwork alone—'

Chloe stomped her foot and moved menacingly

towards the captain. 'Then you tell them that her Royal Highness, Queen of the Universe, Twinkle Twinkle Moo Moo is ordering them to let that planet go!' she screamed.

'Did you say "Twinkle Twinkle Moo Moo"?' said the captain, a little confused.

I shook my head dramatically.

'No …' said Chloe, stopping in her tracks. I mouthed the correct name to her, but it isn't the easiest name to say.

'I meant, of course … Tinkle Tinkle Choo Choo …'

I shook my head even harder and tried one more time.

'Silly me. I mean, my name is of course … Tanka … Tanka … Poo Poo?' she said as if it was a question. It was no use, the jig was up.

'Seize her,' said the captain, looking at Glob. Glob stared back. Seizing wasn't something he was particularly good at. The captain took Chloe by the arm. 'Impersonating the Queen is a crime punishable by eternal tickling, you know?'

'That doesn't sound too bad,' said Chloe, a little relieved. They all say that when they hear the punishment, but being tickled for ever is actually quite horrible indeed.

The captain's hand began to slip off Chloe, and he noticed she was covered in gloop. 'Some sort of disguising agent,' he said, wiping it off until Chloe was revealed in her true form. 'A human, trying to escape, no doubt. No matter, we will put her back on Earth so she can be recycled with the rest of her stupid little planet.'

'No ... you CAN'T! Leave my planet alone! It's my home,' shouted Chloe as she fought back tears.

'Really amazing what technology can do these days, isn't it?' the captain said. 'The recycling of an entire planet in just twenty-four hours! We use the most advanced technology in the Universe. Well, the second-most advanced; it's not exactly Vansarian Tech, but other than Tanka Tanka Woo Woo, who gets to use that?! Or should I say Twinkle Twinkle Moo Moo!' The captain laughed uncontrollably.

I stepped towards him and he pulled out a laser gun and shook his head with a smile.

'I wouldn't do that if I were you,' he said.

I placed my hands in the air, palms facing outwards and stepped back. 'Sorry. Please, I won't do anything, I promise.'

'Let me go! Let my planet go!' said Chloe, hitting the captain with her free arm.

'Chloe, don't,' I said.

'But he DESTROYED my planet!'

'I know, but why hit him when you could just as easily make him a nice hot pizza ...' I said, nodding my head towards the control panel, which was right next to her.

'Great idea! One pepperoni projectile coming right up!' she said, before stamping on the captain's foot, slamming her fist on the control panel and throwing herself to the floor, breaking free from his grip.

The pizza hit the captain in the face and he tumbled over Glob, causing them to both roll around in pizza sauce. I ran over to the control panel and a BLEEP,

BLOOP, BLOP later *Old Faithful* ejected both the
captain and Glob out of the ship.

'Well done, Chloe!' I said, sitting down in the
captain's chair.

'That's "Your Royal Highness" to you,' Chloe said with
a smile.

I smiled back at her. 'Sorry, Your Majesty. Now, let's
get out of here before they get back to their ship.'

I pushed a few buttons, pulled a few levers and *Old
Faithful* purred into action.

And faster than you can say whiiiiiiiisshhhhoooooop,
we were gone.

BOB'S YOUR UNCLE

We pulled on to the nearest hyperspace byway and glided through the stars. It never failed to move me, seeing the flickering of a never-ending stream of planets whooshing by in an instant. It was even more special seeing it through the eyes of someone who had never been into space before.

Chloe sat in my captain's chair, her head resting in her hands, staring into the endless wonder of the Universe. For the slightest moment it allowed her to forget everything that had happened to her that day.

After a few more minutes she let out a huge sigh.

'Are you *sure* we're safe?' she asked, for what felt like

the hundredth time. I didn't mind; I was grateful for any chance to reassure her.

'Yes, we are safe. *Old Faithful* wouldn't allow anyone to track her. We are like a dog in the rain,' I said.

'What, wet?' she said, looking at her dry clothing, a little confused.

'Uh … yes, obviously the dog would be wet. But no, it's a common phrase in the Universe. You see, when dogs get wet, they disappear, just like we have.'

'Um, no they don't,' said Chloe firmly.

'Um, yes they do,' I said, mimicking her tone.

'Not on my planet,' Chloe replied.

'Well, the rain on your planet must really suck then. Poor dogs, nothing they love more than playing hide and seek in the rain on *most* other planets,' I added.

Chloe stared blankly at me then jumped to her feet and clapped her hands purposefully. 'Right, enough of that. We need a plan!' she said, clapping her hands a second time while jogging and punching the air in front of her.

I wasn't entirely sure how punching the air was going

to help, but it seemed to give her focus. A little selfishly, I had thought about suggesting we head back to Empathia. What better proof was there to show them all that the Universe was NOT OK than a life form who had lost their entire planet?

Chloe, however, was determined to come up with a plan to save Earth. We had less than twenty hours now. I wasn't sure how we could possibly help, so Chloe suggested we just throw out the first idea that came into our heads, going back and forth with no judgement.

We mostly ended up arguing over phrases like 'Bob's your uncle', a stupid Earth phrase Chloe seemed to finish EVERY single one of her plans with, despite me telling her countless times that my uncle isn't called Bob. We didn't come up with any good plans but we did manage a few laughs. Chloe was pretty great and we got on like a house on fire.*

She laughed when I suggested we distract the captain by painting 'The Spaceship' all over the side of his ship and then try and take over the controls. I

---

* Another stupid Earth phrase Chloe used. Where I come from, a house being on fire is a BAD thing, but from what I could tell, people on Earth actually became FRIENDS when it happened, or something like that. I can't really remember. Anyway, it's a floo floo phrase.

laughed when she suggested we get a really big leaf blower and blow Earth out of the back of the ship.

However, we didn't come up with anything that was even close to resembling a useable idea. I kept going back to this thought of getting the ship to sick up Earth, but the more I thought about it, the more ridiculous it sounded.

Not knowing much about alien technology, Chloe had run round my ship tirelessly picking up objects and showing them to me before saying, 'Would THIS make a ship sick up a planet?' The answer was always no, but that didn't stop her. She even asked if my toilet roll would do it.

By the time Chloe came into my room to start another round of ideas, I was utterly exhausted. Chloe, on the other hand, was still punching the air, full of boundless energy and determination.

'Look, Chloe ...' I paused, unsure of how to tell her that there was simply no hope of saving Planet Earth.

'POOOEEEEE, I stink!' said Chloe, getting a whiff of her underarm as she punched a little higher.

'That's just space. Stinks, doesn't it?' I said. Then Chloe aimed her air punches towards me and I got a waft of her stench. 'On second thoughts …'

'Does this tin can have a shower?' asked Chloe, banging the dashboard again. This time she managed to set off my glitter cannons, covering the entire deck in glitter.

'Please stop doing that,' I said, wiping the glitter from my eyes.

'Why do you even have glitter cannons?'

'In case I ever have something to celebrate. Not happened yet. Now, you definitely need a shower,' I said, pointing towards a small cubicle at the other end of the room.

While Chloe showered, I brushed off the glitter, set my robotic cleaners to work and then sat in my captain's chair to have one last think about Earth. I knew that *The Spaceship* was incredibly advanced, so in order to break Earth free we would need some pretty Zoop, Zap, Zop tech. I wished the REAL Tanka Tanka Woo Woo had been on my ship earlier. She has the only ship in the Universe powered by Vansarian Tech and that would be zonking helpful about now.

Nope, it was useless. Short of bumping into the Queen of the Universe herself, I was completely out of ideas. I was ready to tell Chloe that when she came out of the shower. I felt awful. Not only had I caused her planet to be swallowed up, but I couldn't think of a way to save it. It was the longest fifteen minutes of my life waiting for her.

'Better?' I said when she finally emerged.

'Much,' she said with a smile. Then she sniffed the air and scrunched up her face as if she'd just inhaled a skonkle fart.* 'Then again …' She sniffed her armpit.

'It's space, trust me. It absolutely reeks!' I said.

She ignored me and walked over. She hesitated, then gave me a big sniff.

'In that case, you stink of space,' she said to me.

I gave myself a sniff. She was right. I smelt zunking awful!

I used it as an excuse to delay telling her that Earth was doomed, and headed for the shower.

---

* If a skonkle plop is the worst kind of poo in the Universe, you can imagine that a skonkle fart doesn't smell very nice at all. Inhaling the gas will almost certainly knock you out, and most likely permanently damage your sense of smell.

I got in and pressed the button.

'ARRRRRRRRGGHHHHHHH,' I screamed, running out of the shower holding my head.

'Mylan, what's wrong with you?!' said Chloe, running after me.

'What's wrong with *me*; what's wrong with YOU?' I screamed. No sooner had the water hit my head than I felt like I was on fire. 'You go into an Empathian's shower and turn the water to HOT?!' I said.

'You go on to a human's planet, misdial an ice cream shop and get the world DESTROYED?!' she screamed back at me. One thing was for sure, you did not beat Chloe Harrison in an argument.

She caught up with me and had to stifle a laugh when she saw me. I was standing in the middle of the flight deck, although I pretty much took up the entire area, I had ballooned so much. As you will recall from the tea episode, hot water and Empathians do not go well together. When it hits our skin, we inflate. As I'd been in a hot shower, my entire body had ballooned and I was now seven feet wide as well as seven feet tall.

However, I didn't care about my body, it was my hair that I was most worried about ...

'Tell me, how bad is it,' I asked meekly and with a bit of a lisp through my inflated lips.

'Um ... Well, you're looking a little chubby,' said Chloe.

'Not my body, my HAIR!' I screamed.

'Oh ...' said Chloe, looking up at my head. She didn't need to say any more. I could feel her surprise. I began to sob. She walked over to me and tried to place a comforting arm around me. She couldn't reach. She headed over to the control deck and a BEEP, BLOOP, BLOP later, she had activated zero-gravity mode. She floated up towards my head where she was able to get both her arms around me. 'Don't worry, Mylan. Everything is going to be OK.'

Eventually I plucked up the courage to check myself out in the reflection of the window. Half of my hair was burnt off! My perfect hair! Gone! I couldn't believe it. 'It could be worse,' said Chloe as she floated back towards the control deck to turn off the zero gravity.

'How?' I said, as I dropped to the ground and began to bounce like a basketball.

'You could have lost ALL your hair,' she said. 'I could cut some of mine off if you like. You know, in solidarity.' She scooped up a big chunk of her hair and mimed a snipping motion with her fingers.

'NO, please! No more senseless crimes against hair,' I said.

Chloe was trying her best to comfort me. It was only a few hours ago that I was desperate to console her for the loss of her planet. Now she was helping me mourn the loss of my hair. I honestly don't know which was worse.*

'It's all going to be OK,' said Chloe, passing me the tub of oil I had instructed her to get from my room. I hoped it would bring the swelling down. I rubbed the oil on my skin and I began to deflate almost instantly. Sadly, the oil didn't bring back my hair though.

'What an awful day,' I said, my hand touching the bald spot for the first of many times.

'Don't suppose you know of any hairdressers around

---

* OK, OK. Having read this back I feel the need to add a note here. I am very much aware that losing a planet is WAY worse than half a head of hair, which will grow back. But at the time I was really hurting, so don't judge me, all right?!

these parts?' said Chloe, trying to lighten the mood.

I jumped to my feet and began bouncing around. Chloe joined me, although she had no idea why we were jumping. We were really starting to be in sync.

'YES!' I shouted.

'YES!' Chloe repeated, before adding, 'Why yes? And why are we jumping?!'

'A hairdresser's; that will solve EVERYTHING,' I screamed, jumping even higher.

'Wow, must be some hairdresser's if it can fix burnt-off hair,' said Chloe.

'No, not that. Although obviously that too. I NEED to get my locks fixed, but that's not what I meant. I know how to save Planet Earth.'

'YOU DO?!' Chloe jumped higher still and began punching the air again.

'I do. *Old Faithful*, set course for Planet K'POW!'

I NEED TO FIX
MY HAIR!

'But ... that's here!' said Flobble, wobbling frantically in excitement.

'Yes,' I said with a smile.

'That means this awful day you've been describing is actually ... TODAY?!'

'It is,' I said.

'That means we're part of it!' said Flobble, somehow reaching a new level of excitement. 'Oooh, I wonder who will play me in the movie!'

'And that means that Earth ... How long since *The Spaceship* swallowed the planet?' asked Heather with a real sense of purpose.

I glanced at my watch. 'Sixteen hours,' I said. The moment the captain had told me how long was left on the countdown I had synchronised my watch so I could keep an eye on the time.

'Then it could still be saved!' she added.

'Look, it's just not possible. I have thought of a million different ideas, but there is no way to save Planet Earth,' I said, standing up.

'But you said you had a plan to save Earth,' said Blurgh, clearly retelling the story in his head. 'Set course for Planet K'POW, you said.'

'I did.' I sighed heavily and walked over to the empty salon seat in front of Heather and sat down. I wrapped the protective blanket around me and adjusted the chair myself so I was at the perfect hair-cutting height. 'But there is simply no saving Planet Earth. It's just me and an Earthling with a tiny, inferior ship, going up against a dark and sinister planetary recycling agency. There is just no way.'

'But then why did you tell her there was?!' said Blurgh angrily.

'Because once she finally understood there was no saving Planet Earth, I knew she would be in floods of tears for DAYS.'

'Of course. Poor girl, losing her home like that,' said Flobble.

'Yeah, poor girl,' I said in agreement. 'BUT if she still had hope, I knew that she could soldier on for a little longer.'

'But why would you want her to hold on any longer than she had to?' asked Flobble.

'Isn't it obvious? I need to fix my hair!' I cried, gesturing at my bald patch.

Flobble and Blurgh gasped and wobbled so furiously that the shop physically shook as if there had been an earthquake.

'You SELFISH ... DECEITFUL ... HORRIBLE ...' said Heather, pressing a button on the chair that ejected me, sending me flying across the room. I landed with a thump on the floor.

I looked up at Heather. 'Does that mean you WON'T cut my hair, because I really want to be looking my best when I tell Chloe—'

Heather came storming over to me, a pair of scissors in each of her hands, her diamond eyes piercing through me.

'Tell me what, exactly?' said Chloe.

Everyone turned round to see Chloe Harrison standing in the doorway. They all froze.

'I … Uh, Chloe … I thought we agreed you would stay on the ship,' I said.

'I didn't agree to anything; you TOLD me to wait on the ship.'

Heather gave me a little kick.

'I'm just surprised to see you,' I said.

'Why, because you programmed the ship to keep me on board no matter what?'

Heather kicked me again.

'Um … No, clearly I didn't because you are here.'

Chloe folded her arms. 'No thanks to you. *Old Faithful* and I got talking and once I told her what you had done to my planet, she let me out.'

I sensed the kick coming this time and rolled to the

side and got to my feet.

'Well, it's great to see you,' I said, moving to the back of the room. Everyone's eyes were fixed on Chloe. For them it was like seeing the characters in a book come to life.

'Anyway, tell me what?' she said strongly.

I took another step back. 'That ... I'm next in the queue?'

'You most certainly are NOT,' said Heather.

'Tell me WHAT?!' Chloe demanded, moving towards me.

'Tell her!' said Heather, who was now also moving towards me. This led to everyone else in the salon joining in.

'I ... uh ... I LIED! OK? I knew you would be really upset when you finally realised Earth can't be saved, and I wouldn't be able to get to a hairdresser's for days until you got over it. So I told you the way to save Earth was at the best hairdresser's in the Universe, on Planet K'POW.' I hung my head in shame.

Chloe looked at me with a wide-eyed fury that was

unmatched by anyone or anyTHING I had ever seen. It was truly remarkable. Everyone could see she was at absolute breaking point. Then I added …

'To be honest, I'm surprised you didn't work it out. Thought you were a bit smarter than the average human.'

Chloe charged at me, landing a heavy blow to my stomach. I went flying into the shelves at the back of the room, knocking everything off them, including a few incredibly valuable Vansarian Tech hairdryers.

'YOU LIAR!' said Chloe, channelling all her anger at the loss of her planet at me. She pulled me up by my shirt, which by the size of her didn't seem possible, then pushed me towards the front of the salon.

'I thought we were becoming friends, that you ACTUALLY cared for me and my planet, but all you care about is your STUPID hair.'

'Hey, that's a bit uncalled for,' I said, getting angry too. I realised that no one was going to agree with me. Sorry, but I just don't like people insulting my hair!

'You are a terrible Empathian, Mylan Bletzleburger, and I never want to see you AGAIN!'

Then Chloe Harrison ran out of The Chop crying, on to an alien planet, all alone.

I took one look at the damage our little fight had caused and all of the angry faces looking at me. I placed a big chunk of money on the side (more than enough to cover the damage) and went towards the door.

'So, just to confirm, there's absolutely no way I can get a haircut?' I said. I was hit by about fifteen different objects as I left the salon.

I picked up the pace as soon as I stepped out of the door. In seconds I was practically running towards my ship. When I arrived, Chloe was waiting for me next to *Old Faithful*.

'Well?' she said expectantly, no sign of the tears that had been streaming down her face moments before.

'You were good,' I said plainly. I didn't want to give her too much of an ego. 'Calling my hair stupid was a bit unnecessary and pushing me into the wall was a bit harsh,' I said, rubbing my shoulder, which was still sore.

'I was in the moment, sorry. Do you think they bought it?' asked Chloe with a hint of a smile forming.

'Absolutely. No one suspected a thing!'

'And did you get it?'

'Of course I did!' I said, reaching triumphantly into my coat pocket. Only there was nothing there. I fumbled around in my pocket, but it was empty.

'Looking for this, Mr Bletzleburger?' said a voice from behind me.

I turned round to see Heather holding a Vansarian Tech hairdryer. It must have fallen out of my pocket.

Chloe and I looked at each other. We had been rumbled.

'Um ...' I said, not sure of what to say.

Chloe looked at me, shaking her head in disappointment. 'Seriously, Mylan, you had ONE job!'

'You know, on Planet K'POW the penalty for stealing is life imprisonment,' Heather said casually. 'BUT the punishment for stealing from the Queen of the Universe is death,' she said, swinging the hairdryer by its wire freely.

'Good thing we didn't steal it off her then!' I said, a little relieved.

'I wouldn't be so sure ...' said Heather, rubbing her face on her sleeve. At first nothing happened, but then I started to see a gloopy substance coming off and her appearance began to change.

Moments later, Her Royal Highness, Queen of the Universe, Tanka Tanka Woo Woo was standing right in front of us.

HER ROYAL HIGHNESS, QUEEN OF THE UNIVERSE

I was in complete shock.

Firstly, I really thought we had got away with it in The Chop. Everything had gone according to plan.

You see, my hair needing to be fixed reminded me of a conversation I'd had with a fellow intergalactic traveller about our passion for all things hair. They had told me about the best haircut they had EVER had, and how the hairdresser had a Vansarian-powered hairdryer.

I knew the only way to save Earth was access to superior technology, and I thought if I could get hold of some Vansarian Tech, then we still had a chance!

But we couldn't just walk in and ask for it. No one in their right mind would believe us, let alone lend us a piece of kit more valuable than *Old Faithful* herself! So we devised a plan. I would tell the people in the salon my story, then Chloe would enter and we would argue, giving me enough time to swipe a hairdryer in the chaos and go and save Planet Earth.

Chloe had been magnificent; she really was a great actress. I couldn't believe Heather had figured it out. But that was NOTHING compared to my surprise that Heather was in fact Tanka Tanka Woo Woo. I could see that the substance she had removed with her sleeve was gloop. Of course, the Queen of the Universe would know all about gloop!

'But you're ... You're ...' I said, unable to form the words. 'Your ... hair is MAGNIFICENT,' I eventually managed, dropping to my knees. It really was. Pictures didn't do it justice. Her hair was a one-of-a-kind masterpiece, a vibrant purple that resembled an impossibly endless waterfall. Her hair seemed to splash on to her shoulders, in a never-ending stream of purple water. It defied gravity, and was befitting of royalty.

'I know,' she stated simply.

'This is the Queen of the Universe, the one you are always going on about? Tanka Tanka Moo Moo?' said Chloe in what was a very disrespectful tone.

'I'm sorry about her, Your Royal Highness—' I started, but Chloe interrupted me.

'If you're the Queen, why are you working in a salon?'

'Being the Queen of the Universe is a very stressful job. Every now and then I like to take a few moments for myself,' said Tanka, flicking her hair over her shoulder. I watched on in awe.

'Cutting hair?' said Chloe, still probing.

'Yes. It calms me. The location of my palace must remain secret for security reasons, so I thought I would build it underneath a salon, on a planet full of salons, as no one would ever think to look there. Then, if I was ever feeling stressed, I could pop up and cut some hair for half an hour. That's what I was doing today, and now I am feeling even MORE stressed than usual.'

'Oooh, you could cut my hair if you're stressed!' I said without thinking. She shot me a look that rivalled the one Chloe had given me in the salon earlier. 'Sorry, forgot the situation we are in for a second there.'

'Yes, it is a difficult situation we are in,' said Tanka, gently stroking the top of the hairdryer. 'Over the years many people have tried to steal my Vansarian Tech, even on a few occasions right here from my salon.

However, I have never heard such a ridiculous story
to cover up an awful and obvious attempt at stealing.
I mean, I saw you try and put the hairdryer in your
pocket three times while you lay on the floor, then you
dropped it as you stood up and didn't even realise. It
was remarkably terrible.'

Chloe shot me another disapproving look. 'REALLY,
Mylan, you DROPPED it?! We could have been out of
here by now, actually saving my planet.' Chloe began to
fidget, looking at her wrist despite not wearing a watch.
She knew that time was against us.

'Earth? Empathia? ULRA? A planet-eating spaceship
called *The Spaceship*? That weird tea drink ... You
expect me to believe all of that is true?!' said Tanka,
trying to stifle a laugh.

'YES!' said Chloe, taking a step towards her. She really
was fearless for someone so small.

'You expect me to believe—'

'No, I expect you to hand over that hairdryer, as
someone here is incapable of slipping it into a pocket
...' She glanced at me out of the corner of her eye and

shook her head disapprovingly again. 'So that we can SAVE my planet!'

'You are quite the fiery little creature, aren't you?' said Tanka. It was hard to tell if she was offended or impressed.

'Sorry, she can be a right little chunka dunk,'* I said, trying to save her from being executed on the spot.

Tanka looked at Chloe. 'So he really *did* recycle your planet while trying to order ice cream?' she said.

'*Destroyed* not recycled, and yes. If it's any consolation, the more I hear it, the more ridiculous it sounds to me too,' said Chloe.

Tanka Tanka Woo Woo nodded her head and paused for thought. After what felt like the longest pause I had ever encountered (and I once visited a planet where the life forms would pause after every ... single ... word ... that ... they ... said. It was incredibly .... frustrating!) she finally spoke.

'Perhaps this is a case of a story being too weird not to be true,' said the Queen of the Universe, who, to my

---

* A chunka dunk is a squirrel-like creature found on the Planet Chardog. It is thought to be the cheekiest species in the entire Universe. It spends its life setting up traps all over the forest, so that when people go there to have a picnic, dastardly things happen to them. The chunka dunks then steal the picnic, and eat it in front of the people they've stolen it from. They are little rascals!

amazement, handed the hairdryer to Chloe.

'Great! So we're free to go?' said Chloe, taking a step towards my ship and grabbing me by the hand.

'Of course …' said Tanka, but I could tell she was about to add something (you don't spend three weeks living on a planet with life forms that pause after every word without picking up on when someone has more to say). I turned to face *Old Faithful* in the hope I could speed her up a little. It worked. 'But, Mylan … how exactly do you intend to take down an entire spaceship with a hairdryer?'

'That's EXACTLY what I asked!' said Chloe. 'Give me a high-five, sister!' Chloe held out her hand at Tanka Tanka Woo Woo, who looked a little confused.

'It's an Earth ritual,' I said.

'I see,' said Tanka, holding her hand up in the same pose without touching Chloe's. She put her hand down. 'Ooh, I like that, it's fun!'

'I asked him a hundred times on the way over here, how are you going to save an entire planet with a hairdryer, but he kept saying things like, "You don't understand space travel ... blah ... blah ... blah"', said Chloe with a smug smile.

'Yes, well, you *don't* understand space travel,' I said.

'Yes, well, I DO understand space travel, Mylan, and I am excited to hear your explanation,' said Tanka, taking the hairdryer from Chloe and putting it in my hands.

For a moment I forgot her question and simply stared at the hairdryer, in awe of the incredible craftsmanship. You could tell it really was extremely advanced technology.

'Well ...' I said, turning it over in my hands. 'I was going to figure it out on the way there,' I confessed feebly.

'Give that here,' said Tanka, forcefully removing it from my hand.

'Hey, what are you doing?!' Chloe went to grab the hairdryer back, but Tanka Tanka Woo Woo was remarkably agile, dodging her effortlessly.

'I'm going to do what this silly little boy should have done hours ago,' said Tanka.

'Am I the silly little boy?' I asked.

'And what's that?' asked Chloe.

'I'm going to help you save your planet. Now, follow me; we don't have much time,' said Tanka Tanka Woo Woo, who smiled for the very first time since I met her. It didn't last long however. The Queen of the Universe spun round with purpose and moved away from my spaceship at pace. Chloe ran along behind her.

'Uh ... Your Royal Highness ...' I began.

She didn't look back. 'If you think I would be caught dead in that rusty old spaceship of yours ...' she said dismissively. I glanced over at *Old Faithful* and was offended on her behalf. For the average intergalactic traveller, she was a fine spaceship indeed. However, Her Royal Highness Tanka Tanka Woo Woo, Queen of the Universe was NOT your average intergalactic traveller. This point was made even clearer to me as she stopped outside her ship. It was INCREDIBLE. Twin-turbo hypersonic engines; dynamic, bi-folding alloy-trim wings; super-duper pea-wee shooter cannons (they may not sound particularly impressive, but they were the BEST defensive weapons you could buy!) and of course it was …

'Jet black,' said Tanka, putting a hand on her ship fondly. 'All the greatest ships are, of course.'

'Of course,' I said, trying not to sound impressed.

'Close your mouth, Mylan, you're dribbling,' said Chloe. Unfortunately we Empathians have weak jaws, and when we are surprised they fall open and it takes a couple of minutes for them to slowly close back up.

We entered the ship and everything inside was jet black too, with dim purple lighting leading the way to the captain's deck, where there were three chairs. That was all. I have seen some ships with minimalist designs before, but I couldn't even see any controls. I clearly looked puzzled.

'Vansarian Tech,' said Tanka proudly. 'Perfectly designed for its purpose and so simple, even a complete buffoon could use it. That's actually their slogan, you know.'

'Wait, even Mylan? We are talking about someone who struggles to make a simple phone call to an ice cream shop,' said Chloe. Tanka smiled once more and nodded. I ignored the insult; I was too excited by what I was seeing or, more accurately, what I *couldn't* see.

'This is absolutely incredible,' I said, running my fingers along the back of the plush leather chair. I felt a pang of guilt as I dreamt of owning a ship like this one day. How would poor *Old Faithful* feel?! 'I've always wanted to be on a Vansarian-powered ship.'

'Van-SAIR-ian, not Van-SAR-ian,' said Tanka.

'Sorry, my bad. So how does it work?' I said.

'It's easy. You simply state your destination, close your eyes, hold your breath and count to three.'

'And?' I asked.

'You have arrived,' said Tanka plainly.

'Intergalactic teleportation? I thought that was just a myth! I know we can transport people a short distance, a few miles tops, but across the entire Universe?!' My mouth fell open again. I tried to push it back up, but I was too amazed by this news.

'That's what the Vansarians do. Take a simple concept and perfect it. Then give it to me and no one else.'

'Why do you need to close your eyes and hold your breath?' asked Chloe. I was wondering the same thing.

'Travelling trillions of miles across time and space in the blink of an eye can give you a bit of a headache if you don't prepare yourself. I don't suppose you'd like to give it a go?' Tanka Tanka Woo Woo said.

My eyes lit up. I couldn't believe it, a chance to pilot a Vansarian-powered spaceship capable of intergalactic teleportation. Abso-zunking-lutely!

'Sure, sounds fun! Spaceship, take me to Earth,' said Chloe quickly.

'Earth NOT FOUND,' said a voice.

'Does that mean ...' asked Chloe in horror.

'Not necessarily. Mylan, how much longer do we have?' asked Tanka, sounding concerned.

I looked at my watch. 'A little over seven hours,' I said.

'It probably can't locate your planet inside *The Spaceship*. Don't worry, that's not where we need to go first anyway,' said Tanka.

'Where are we going?' I asked.

'Vansaria,' she said coolly, as if visiting the most exclusive and elusive planet in the known Universe wasn't a big deal. 'I was heading there anyway. I need to refuel and Vansaria is the only place I can do that.'

'And then we will head back to the giant spaceship to save my home?' asked Chloe.

'Exactly. Right after we get the Vansarians to create something that can save your planet. Something powerful but simple to use! Time is tight, so we'd best be on our way. Mylan, would you like to do the honours?' The Queen of the Universe pointed towards the captain's chair and, for the first time, smiled at me directly.

I couldn't believe it. After all the terrible things that had gone wrong, finally something Zoop, Zap, Zop was happening. The Queen of the Universe was asking me to pilot the most powerful and impressive ship in the Universe!

I sat down and an overwhelming feeling of positivity washed over me. In that moment, I knew that we were going to save Earth, reunite Chloe with her family and convince every Empathian to follow me into the great unknown, helping every life form we encountered along the way. It was an incredible feeling ...

And it lasted for roughly three seconds.

CUSTOMERS!

'Spaceship ... take us to Vansaria,' I said as I closed my eyes, held my breath and counted to three.

Intergalactic teleportation was an odd feeling. I felt a pulse through my chest, which ran up through my neck and down my spine simultaneously, followed by a high-pitched screeching and a low hum. It felt like someone had spun me round really fast on a wheelie chair and then kicked it over.

Then silence. Stillness. I opened my eyes, looked out of the window and could see we were no longer on K'POW. I must admit, my first impressions of Vansaria were underwhelming. I had envisaged a metropolis of skyscrapers with luxurious swimming pools everywhere and glorious sunshine glaring down from three different suns.

What I saw was a dank, dark and grimy planet, with a tiny shack in the centre and not a whole lot else. And it was raining. A LOT. Who was I to question the Vansarian people though? It obviously worked for them, although perhaps they should think about using some of their technology to brighten up their own planet.

I turned towards Tanka and Chloe with a beaming smile to hide any reservations I had and was met with crossed arms and frowning faces. They were standing in the exact same pose. It was scary. It was at this point I tuned in and sensed their burning anger.

'He's done it again, hasn't he?!' said Chloe.

'Yep,' replied Tanka shortly.

'Done what exactly?' I said.

'Messed everything up,' said Tanka, rubbing her eyes.

'I don't understand,' I said, looking out of the window once again.

'It's Van-SAIR-ia not Van-SAR-ia,' said Chloe, pointing towards the shack.

'Even the Earthling gets it, and life forms on that backward little planet don't even know I exist! No offence,' said Tanka.

'None taken,' said Chloe, holding up her hand for a high-five. Tanka put hers up and then placed it down by her side again.

I looked towards the shack and read the rusting neon sign:

VANS ARE HERE

'Vans are here,' I said. 'Vans … are … 'ere,' I repeated. 'Vans … ar … ia. Vansaria. Oh, dear …' I fell to my knees, ready to burst into tears, but Tanka grabbed me by my arm as I fell and hoisted me back up.

'My fault,' she said as she dusted me off. 'You spent ages telling me how you always mess things up and that you essentially destroyed an entire planet because you misdialled a phone number, and I let you pilot my ship. That's on me. Crying on the floor isn't going to get us off this planet. We need fuel,' she said, and she

182

opened up the door and began walking to the little shack.

'Come on, we've no time to lose,' said Chloe, grabbing me by the hand and pulling me towards the door.

'Wait, Chloe!' I said, pulling her back. 'Probably worth a top-up.' I pulled out my BREATHE dispenser. She sighed heavily. I had given her a dose before she left the ship on K'POW and she had said it tasted awful. She hesitated and I reminded her, 'You need it to breathe ...'

She rolled her eyes and opened her mouth. We both swallowed a bubble (I think it actually tastes pretty nice, just like a chalk and cheese sandwich!) and we followed after Tanka, who seemingly had no problem breathing. She probably used some form of Vansarian Tech.

No sooner had we touched the surface of the planet, we were greeted by a young alien.

He was a cute little thing. He was yellow, had a perfectly square body, a pear-shaped head with one big eye, and ten arms that were far too long for his body. He stared at us, unblinking.

Tanka smiled at him. 'Hello, my name is Tanka Tanka Woo Woo, Queen of the Universe and we need some assistance.'

Nothing. The boy just stared.

'Uh ... hello?' said Chloe, waving at him.

Still nothing.

'Are you on your own here, little buddy?' I said.

'CUSTOMERS!!!!' he screamed at the top of his voice. 'CUSTOMERS!!!' he yelled again, turning to face the shack. He began running towards it, all ten of his arms flailing in the wind as he ran, shouting 'CUSTOMERS!' over and over. As he got closer, I could hear another voice.

'Customers?!' it seemed to echo in surprise. A pear-shaped head popped up at the top window. 'CUSTOMERS!' it screamed back.

'We haven't bought anything yet,' said Chloe, a little fed up of having CUSTOMERS shouted at her.

Moments later, the older alien was running out

of the door. He scooped the little alien up in his arms as he ran towards us, all the while screaming 'CUSTOMERS!' right at us. I have been to many shops across the Universe and I had never encountered such an enthusiastic welcome. For a fleeting second I felt their overwhelming delight at seeing other living life forms and it filled my heart with joy.

'My name is Customers!' said the creature, who looked exactly like the young alien he held in his hands, with the addition of a whopping big moustache and a cowboy hat. 'Sorry, I mean Drex, my name is Drex. Been a while since we've had customers so please excuse my excitement! A very long while, in fact.'

'CUSTOMERS!' shouted the young alien.

'That's right, little one! I can't wait to tell your mumma! "*No one will ever buy anything all the way out here. You'll be lucky if you get a single customer EVER.*" Well, look who's laughing now? 480 years later and BOOM! Our FIRST EVER CUSTOMERS!!' he shouted, doing a victory dance.

'CUSTOMERS!' said the young alien again.

'Uh ... what exactly do you sell?' I said cautiously.

'VANS!' shouted Drex, unable to contain his excitement.

'Vans?' said Chloe, a little confused. 'Don't all you space travellers use spaceships?'

FOR SALE!

'Absolutely, little lady. VANS stands for "Very Average Normal Spaceships". TA-DA!!' he said, swivelling around and pointing all of his arms towards half a dozen rusty old spaceships parked outside the shack.

'Yes, well, I'm afraid we may have arrived here by mistake,' said Tanka.

'Best mistake you ever made!' said the young alien in a dramatically deep voice as he jumped down from his dad's arms and offered out one of his ten hands. I shook it politely. 'The name's Drex Junior,' he continued, suddenly finding his voice. 'Trainee sales assistant here at VANS Are Here, your number-one choice for very average, normal spaceships.'

'What is going on?' asked Chloe. It was a fair question.

'What's going on is I'm about to make you a great deal on one heck of an average and incredibly normal spaceship,' said Drex Junior, looking at his dad for approval. He received ten thumbs-up and a beaming smile.

'We are NOT looking to buy one of your rusty old

buckets! Have you seen the ship we arrived on?' said Tanka, getting frustrated. Chloe walked over to one of the very average, normal spaceships and gave it a light tap. A cloud of dust blew in her face. Not even BREATHE could stop her from choking as she inhaled.

'A little too black, if you ask me. Have you considered something a little more rusty in colour?' said Drex Junior.

'That's my boy! Way to push the sale!' said Drex Senior, standing proudly behind him.

'We don't want to buy one of your AWFUL spaceships. We came here in the most advanced and brilliant spaceship in the entire Universe!' said Chloe.

'We also sell air fresheners,' said Drex Junior, receiving a hearty pat on the back from his dad.

'One sniff of this planet and I can tell it would be a bad idea to get an air freshener from here,' said Tanka. She was right, the stench was awful. She turned her back on the Drexes to face me and Chloe. 'We don't have much time and we need to get to *The Spaceship* to save Planet Earth.'

'This is taking too long!' said Chloe desperately.

'Right,' I agreed. 'But the ship is out of fuel and, thanks to Mylan, we are not in Vansaria, nor can we get there in time to save Earth.'

'Out of fuel, are you? We have the most incredibly average and normal fuel source ever made right here!' said Drex Junior. He pointed over to a huge mound of what can only be described as manure.

'Yep, that's right. There is roughly 480 years of poop! Powers all of our VANS,' said Drex Senior.

'And makes one heck of an air-freshener fragrance,' said Drex Junior.

THAT'S what the smell was. 480-year-old poop. Believe it or not, this was the third time on my travels I had come across ancient poop being used as an air freshener. I really should have recognised it sooner.

'THAT'S what that smell is. I assumed it was Mylan,' said Chloe, giving me a playful kick.

'My ship does *not* run on poop,' said Tanka Tanka Woo Woo, which caused Chloe to giggle.

'Oh, I see,' said Drex Senior, sounding a little upset.

'So I guess what you're saying is you and that beautiful ship of yours are stuck here?'

'I ... uh ...' said Tanka, at a loss for words. I was secretly quite impressed with Drex Senior; he made a good point.

'You know, we do have some very average, normal spaceships for sale at some incredible prices,' said Drex Junior.

'NO! I am NOT getting in one of those spaceships. I simply refuse!' said Tanka, folding her arms and stamping her foot.

Then I felt it, the total desperation of Drex Junior and his dad. Earlier I had briefly tuned in to their emotions and felt how happy they were to see us. Now I dug a little deeper and I could sense why.

They were hurting.

I could see now that all Drex Senior wanted was one single sale, to prove he hadn't wasted his entire life. They were such a stubborn species that he wouldn't leave this awful, stinking planet until he and his son had sold a spaceship. I felt so sorry for him that I simply couldn't stop the next words from coming out of my mouth.

'We'll take one!' I declared.

'Sorry, what?!' said Tanka. I avoided eye contact with her.

'Sorry, what?!!' said Drex Junior and Senior together.

'Woof! Woof!' Even their dog was surprised. I looked around but couldn't see it. Must have been hiding in the rain, I thought. Chloe remembered what I had said and picked up a stick. She threw it towards the shack and was very happy to see it floating through the air towards her moments later.

'Well, I'll be,' she said, patting the air just above the stick. 'Good boy!'

'I said we'll take one,' I repeated slowly, as everyone seemed to have lost the ability to understand me.

'Mylan …' said Tanka, but I moved away from her and over towards Drex Junior.

'Which one?!' said Drex Junior, jumping up and down with excitement.

'Um … the super-rusty-coloured *rusty* one?'

'EXCELLENT choice!' said Drex Senior, shaking both of my hands, cupping my face with his spare ones. 'I'll take you over to the office where we can draw up the paperwork. Now, have you thought about insurance, because boy-oh-boy are you going to need it for this little beauty.'

After a few minutes I emerged with a set of keys and a box of air fresheners.

'Pleasure doing business with you, Mr Bletzleburger!' said Drex Senior, before embracing his son and running straight back into the shack, where he began packing his belongings hastily.

'What EXACTLY do you think you are doing?!' said Tanka, who as far as I could tell had remained in the exact same pose of enraged fury this entire time.

'Getting us out of here,' I said bluntly, handing Chloe the box of air fresheners. She gave them a sniff and instantly regretted it.

'Can spaceships smell? Because if they can this might make *The Spaceship* sick up Earth; it's disgusting! They smell like ... like ... my brother's farts!'

'I am NOT getting on that ship,' said Tanka.

I looked at Chloe. 'If we don't leave right now, we have no chance of saving Earth. I've calculated the distance and top speed needed to get to *The Spaceship*. If we leave in the next two minutes, we will make it with barely five minutes to spare.'

'This is LUDICROUS. I will simply call for someone from Vansaria to pick us up, refuel the ship and we will get to Earth in plenty of time,' said Tanka, taking out her phone.

'Please, go ahead,' I said, having already checked the signal. Not surprisingly in the back end of nowhere, there was none. Not even for the Queen of the Universe.

'I have no signal,' said Tanka glumly.

'And we have no other options. We must leave right NOW!' I said.

'Well, seems pretty clear to me,' said Chloe, walking quickly towards the ship, struggling awkwardly as she tried to hold her nose at the same time as carrying the box of air fresheners.

'Those things are not coming with us,' said Tanka, finally taking a step towards the ship. 'Why would you buy them anyway; they smell AWFUL.'

'I couldn't resist. They were buy one get one free,' I said.

'Buy one horrible air freshener, get another free. Great deal,' said Chloe sarcastically.

'No, if you bought a box of the air fresheners, you got a spaceship free,' I said as I pressed the button to open the door. It bleeped pathetically and then slowly opened, the rust causing an almighty creaking noise. Chloe gave a gentle tap to the outside of the ship and a large metallic box fell off from underneath it. She looked at me with concern.

'Probably not important,' I said with very little confidence.

'What kind of awful ship is worth less money than a box full of 480-year-old poop-fragranced air fresheners?!' asked Tanka in utter dismay.

'This one,' I said proudly. 'I've called her *Rusty.*'

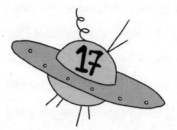

RECYCLING OF PLANET COMPLETE

Chloe entered the ship first and I followed. I looked behind to see the Queen of the Universe, arms folded, rooted to the spot.

'I am NOT getting on that ship with those zunking awful air fresheners,' she said.

'Fine.' I tossed the box out and it landed on the ground. Tanka nodded and then entered the ship. She immediately held her nose.

'WOW!' she said, her face folding up like a stack of newspapers. 'That is DISGUSTING! How could it possibly smell worse on here than it does out there?!'

'That's just what I was thinking,' said Chloe, climbing

out again to pick up the box of 480-year-old poop-fragranced air fresheners. 'I think we might need these.' She brought them in, and Tanka didn't complain.

I sat down in the captain's seat, turned the key in the ignition (yep, this spaceship still used a key!) and put my foot down. As we blasted off, I could see Drex Senior and his son jumping up and down next to their shack. I only caught a glimpse of them for a second or two, but their joy stayed with me long after we left the planet. It radiated out of them far into outer space.

'Hold on, Earth, we're coming!' shouted Chloe, her leg jiggling in excitement.

'Hang a few of those air fresheners in this corner here, would you, Mylan?' said Tanka.

We sped along at a terrifyingly low speed of 88,000 miles per hour (I promise I really did have my foot down. That's as fast as it would go!).

'Won't this thing go any faster?!' said Chloe, bashing at the controls. A nozzle which looked like it should spout water came down from the ceiling and spat dust in my face. Seconds later, a mouldy slice of bread hit me in the face.

'Guess this ship doesn't do pizza. Good thing I'm not peckish,' said Chloe, peeling the green, furry bread off my face.

I put the ship on autopilot and for the first time since leaving planet K'POW I had time to think about the situation I found myself in.

Here I was, on a ship travelling towards a doomed planet in an effort to save it, with the sole survivor of that planet and Her Royal Highness Tanka Tanka Woo Woo. I pinched myself and then I pinched her.

'How dare you touch me!' she said, before giving me an almighty kick.

Yep, it was definitely her. All those years I had spent staring at her picture on my wall back on Empathia, thinking of a thousand questions I would like to ask her (half of which were hair-related), and here I was in a room with her for the next few hours with nothing to do except look out at the stars and hold our noses because of the stench.

'Go on then, ask away,' said Tanka, not even turning

to look at me. She must have sensed my eagerness, or perhaps it was because I had been staring at her with a goofy smile for the past half an hour.

'So you're the Queen of the Universe then?' said Chloe, jumping in first.

'Yes,' said Tanka regally.

'What exactly does that mean? And who put you in charge?' asked Chloe. I was mortified as these were questions not suitable for royal monarchs (although I was desperate to know myself).

'My family have been "in charge", as you put it, since the dawn of time. Although I would say that we were more guardians, in place to protect the Universe rather than to rule it,' said Tanka.

'Cool. Is it fun?' asked Chloe, getting in ahead of me again. I had so many burning questions but they were all getting mixed up in my brain and I couldn't get them out fast enough.

'Sometimes,' said Tanka with a wry smile.

'I bet it is,' said Chloe thoughtfully. 'I bet it's nice being treated so well all the time. I bet no one has ever locked a gate right in front of you because you were thirty seconds late!'

'I can't say that they have,' said Tanka. 'Although I am not always treated so nicely ...' She looked around the ship and frowned.

'Oh, yeah, guess not!' said Chloe.

'Do you not have any questions?' said Tanka, turning towards me. I felt my cheeks flush.

'Oh, he DEFINITELY does! He grew up with a poster of you on his wall!' said Chloe, giggling. Now my cheeks were positively burning.

'You little chunka dunk!' I said, trying to hide my embarrassment.

Tanka smiled. She seemed genuinely amused. 'How about you ask me those questions you asked of your bedroom wall while I fix your hair. What's left of it anyway ...'

'I ... uh ...' I couldn't speak, so Chloe did it for me.

'What he's trying to say is that he's speechless, but he can't say it, you know, because he's—'

'Speechless,' said Tanka with a smile. Seemingly out

of nowhere, she pulled out a set of shining gold scissors and a mirror. She passed me the mirror to hold, and began to chop at my hair effortlessly.

One of the greatest pleasures in life is having your hair cut, but to have it done by the Queen of the Universe herself! It was honestly the best moment of my life. All questions I had vanished away, and I sat in silence as she weaved her magic on my head.

'Hmmmmm,' she said, and the chopping stopped.

'What's wrong? You couldn't possibly make him look any worse!' said Chloe.

'The hair he has now looks fantastic. It's just what to do with this bald patch,' said Tanka, rubbing her chin thoughtfully.

'Can it ... not be fixed?' I asked hesitantly. If Tanka Tanka Woo Woo, the most incredible hairdresser in the Universe (and Queen of it, obviously) couldn't fix it, then I was doomed.

'Yes, of course I can fix it,' she said without hesitation. 'I'm just trying to think of the best way ...'

'Sorry, I didn't mean ... Of course you can fix it! You

have the most wonderful hair in the Universe, after all!'
I said, taking another look at the impossible waterfall
that ran down to her shoulders.

'Get me my hairdryer, and a glass of water,' said the
Queen confidently. 'I know exactly what to do.'

Chloe passed her the Vansarian Tech hairdryer and
fetched a glass of water. I checked to make sure it was
cold. I didn't want to get burnt again!

'Right, Chloe, when I say OK, I want you to throw
that water on Mylan.'

'OK!' said Chloe, throwing the glass of water all over
me. I spluttered.

'Not yet!' said Tanka.

'Oh, sorry. I've got another glass though!' said Chloe.

'OK, great,' said Tanka.

'If you say so ...' Chloe threw the second glass over
me. I spluttered some more.

'NO! You have to wait until I say OK!'

'But you did. Twice, in fact,' said Chloe, who clearly
thought she was being very smart. I wasn't impressed,
but Tanka was smiling.

'I suppose you're right. Perhaps we should go with an old-fashioned three-count,' said Tanka. Chloe filled up the glass, and Tanka prepared the hairdryer and scissors.

'One ... Two ... Three!'

Chloe threw the water and I braced myself for a cold splash to the face again, but it never came. I opened one eye to see something miraculous. The water Chloe

had thrown was suspended in the air just above me. I opened my other eye and could see the hairdryer was holding it in place. Tanka was moving the hairdryer back and forth, lightly snipping at the water and creating waves.

It was the most beautiful thing I had ever seen. Tanka fixed the waves of water to my head to cover the bald patch and stepped back.

'My hair ... My incredible, wonderful, zunking AMAZING hair!' I said, lightly running my fingers through it in disbelief. It was wet to the touch, but my hand dried instantly. My hair resembled a tumbling, impossible waterfall, just like Tanka's. I had never been so grateful in my entire life. 'Thank you, thank you.'

Tanka nodded. Even Chloe was impressed. 'I love it,' she said.

'Vansarian Tech is incredible,' I said, looking at the hairdryer.

Tanka handed it to me. 'Be careful,' she said.

I nodded.

'It really is something,' she said.

'The most astonishing thing I have ever seen,' I said, admiring the craftsmanship as Chloe plonked herself down next to me.

'I don't know, this gloop stuff is pretty awesome,' she said, opening a jar and scooping up a zunking big blob of it in her hand. 'Hey, I wonder what YOU would turn into if I slap this all over you,' she said playfully.

'NO!' screamed Tanka, throwing herself at Chloe and knocking the gloop out of her hand.

'Hey, what are you doing?!' said Chloe, trying to scoop the gloop off the floor.

'Do you have a death wish, girl?' said Tanka sternly.

'I don't think so,' replied Chloe.

'Gloop and Vansarian Tech do NOT play nicely together.'

'Really?' I said.

'I learnt the hard way. You put even a speck of gloop on a piece of Vansarian hardware, and anything could happen, and I mean ANYTHING.'

'Reeeeeeeeallllllly?' I said.

'Worst case, it could explode, destroying everything

within a three-planet radius.'

'Wow!' I said, looking down at the innocent-looking hairdryer.

Tanka crossed her arms and nodded. 'The truth is that something different happens every time they come into contact with each other. They are just not a good mix.'

'What kind of things?' Chloe asked.

'Well, one time I accidentally dropped a speck of it on my Vansarian watch and I turned into a tree the size of a planet for two hours.'

'REMARKABLE!' I screamed with glee.

Tanka took the hairdryer and placed it as far away from me as she could. I made a mental note of where it was in the hope that I could do a couple of tests of my own, you know, as soon as Earth was saved …

As *Rusty* chugged along through the galaxy, Chloe asked me a bunch of questions about one of my favourite subjects. Spaceships! She was impressed that even though I'd never been in this particular model of ship before, I knew how to fly it and, more importantly, how to find Earth.

'It was easy, really,' I said. 'I just reprogrammed the ship's analogue computer with my synco-computo-maximo-3000, setting course for the previous coordinates of Earth, utilising a parameter field that would search for any ship the size of a planet in the vicinity. Then I whacked the ship into autopilot and kicked back. Routine stuff.'

Chloe's jaw dropped open this time. 'That's pretty impressive, though I did make it throw mouldy bread at you, so ...' said Chloe, shrugging her shoulders and raising her eyebrows at me.

A little while later the ship juddered and stuttered out of autopilot, which could only mean one thing: we had arrived. The giant *Spaceship* was still hanging out by Earth's Moon. Hopefully they wouldn't see our tiny craft sneaking up to it.

'Right, we need to get inside,' Chloe said, looking for a way in.

'That's easy,' said Tanka, taking over *Rusty*'s controls and steering it towards some enormous doors in the side of the giant *Spaceship*. 'Get me my hairdryer and a glass of water.'

Tanka told me to hover *Rusty* right next to the doors. She then opened our airlock, leaned out of *Rusty* and threw the glass of water at the doors' control panel. She switched on the hairdryer as the water hit the panel and the water floated there, before completely covering the panel. It stayed there for a second, then numbers began to appear.

'Is that the door code?' I asked in disbelief.

'Easy, see?' she said, punching in the numbers. The huge doors opened to reveal an enormous cargo bay. It was unbelievably large and at the very end, suspended, was Planet Earth.

'Wow,' said Chloe a bit tearily.

Tanka Tanka Woo Woo simply gasped, momentarily speechless.

'It really is so beautiful,' I said, remembering how I'd felt when I had first come across the planet after years of searching. It was the closest thing to seeing my home since leaving Empathia. But it wasn't my home; it

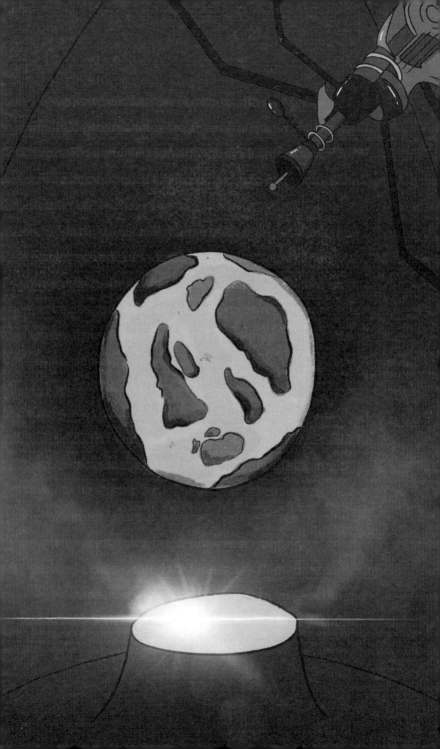

was Chloe's and it was in danger.

Real danger, and it was plain to see. As beautiful as Earth looked as it gently rotated, suspended in the middle of this ginormous spaceship, it was almost entirely covered by an unsettling red haze.

Above Earth, there was a large ray gun, the biggest I had ever seen, emitting a solid red beam that was spreading a red mist across the entire planet. I didn't know what it was, but the fact it was almost complete suggested it was an important part of the recycling process. We had to stop it, but I had no idea how.

I looked at my watch.

'Six minutes,' I said, fighting the urge to continue counting down.

'Quick!' shouted Chloe.

We flew into the cargo bay, landed *Rusty* and ran out into the large empty area.

Tanka Tanka Woo Woo looked around for anything that might help.

'There!' she shouted, pointing towards a solitary control panel.

I ran over to it with her, leaving Chloe staring at her planet being consumed by the red mist. I could feel her pain, her loss, her sense of complete and utter hopelessness, but I had to ignore it, if only for the next …

'Five minutes,' said Tanka, who had synchronised her watch to mine.

We looked down at the control panel to see a single, big red button.

Here's the thing about big red buttons. They are either used for incredibly good things, like turning on Christmas lights, or breathtaking fireworks displays … or they are used for very bad things, like detonating a bomb, or recycling an entire planet.

They are never used for normal things, like turning on a fan or a bedroom light. But the absolute WORST thing about big red buttons …

They were NEVER clearly labelled.

'What does it do?' asked Chloe, who had now joined us, as she looked nervously at the button and then at Planet Earth.

'Something very good, or very bad,' I said, my hand hovering over it cautiously.

'Is there a label?' she said, looking around the control panel. Other than an electric socket, though, there was nothing but the button.

'Don't bother looking; they are never clearly labelled,' I said.

'Do we press it?' asked Chloe, showing incredible restraint considering how much she had messed around with my ship's controls.

'I have no idea!' I said, and then to everyone's surprise (including my own) I slammed my fist down and pressed the button.

At first, nothing happened, which was a little anticlimactic. I stared at Earth, half expecting it to disappear, half hoping the red mist would vanish. Neither of those things happened. Instead, the floor beneath us began to rise.

We began moving slowly, then all of a sudden we whooshed into the air at hyper-speed.

'What's happening?!' Chloe asked, but before I could

answer with 'no idea', an announcement was made over the ship's speakers.

'You have arrived at the captain's deck,' it said.

In front of us was a set of doors made of solid gold. They swung open, and there was the captain and his crew.

'Stop the red laser!' shouted Chloe.

'Who is that in our viewing deck, Glob?' said the captain.

'It looks like the alien who ordered the recycling of the planet we just picked up, sir,' said Glob, rolling towards us to get a better look. 'Yes, it's them, sir,' he confirmed.

'Ah yes! What was his name again? Blingle Booger?'

'Bletzleburger, sir.'

'Ah yes! Neat little trick that puny little spaceship of yours pulled on us. No matter, knew we'd catch up with you eventually,' he said, as if he had captured us. 'And he's not alone.' The captain took a closer look at Chloe and Tanka. 'He's brought back the fugitive and …' The captain smiled when he saw Tanka.

'Someone pretending to be the Queen of the Universe again,' said Glob, not impressed.

'They haven't brought me back to you. This is the ACTUAL Queen of the Universe and WE have come here to save my planet!' said Chloe in a pretty powerful statement, which was ever so slightly weakened by the announcement that followed over the ship's speakers.

'Recycling of planet completion in two minutes.'

I glanced at my watch. It told the same story. Two minutes until Earth was destroyed.

'Oh, I see. I'm afraid you're too late,' said the captain in a tone that sounded full of regret but was lacking in any empathy at all.

'We'll see about that!' said Tanka Tanka Woo Woo, swishing her hair back regally. 'As Queen of the Universe I demand – no, I COMMAND – you to put that planet back where you found it immediately!'

'Haven't we been through this before? Can't be done!' said the captain with just the hint of a smile.

This lit a fire inside Chloe. As far as I know, humans can't catch fire when they are angry (unlike the inhabitants of Planet Pyro), but it was as if there was heat radiating off her. She marched towards the captain, rolling up her sleeves and snarling menacingly.

'PUT ... MY ... PLANET ... BACK!' she screamed, thrashing her hands wildly at the captain in between each word. However, a guard grabbed her before she could reach him, holding her back.

'There is nothing I can do. Your planet will be recycled and be much more valuable to the Universe as a clone planet, I assure you,' said the captain.

'You keep using this word "recycled"! You mean DESTROYED!' said Chloe angrily, wrestling herself free.

The captain, a little fearful, hid behind Glob, and his guards formed a wall between him and Chloe. 'No, recycled. You see, we take all the life force on the planet, smush it all together and it makes excellent, shiny new planets full of life and hope! And clones, lots and lots of clones.'

'Although this is the first time we have ever had a loose end, sir; what do we do about HER?' said Glob, rolling his eyes in Chloe's direction.

'Good point. We don't have time to get her on to the planet now.'

'I don't care what you do with me. I just want to save my home!' Chloe charged with all her might at the wall of guards. She smashed into them, before being wrestled to the ground and subdued.

I felt like I had been punched in the gut. I couldn't breathe. I had finally felt the WORST feeling in the world. The feeling of losing your home. As Chloe lay motionless on the floor, she had finally given up the last sliver of hope she had. I knew I had to do something, ANYTHING, to save Planet Earth.

'Recycling of planet completion in sixty seconds.'

'This is an outrage! I have given you a command, captain!' said Tanka, clearly very frustrated. The captain simply shrugged his shoulders.

I reached into my bag and pulled out the Vansarian-powered hairdryer. 'Nobody move!' I said.

The crew looked uneasy and put up their hands (apart from Glob, for understandable reasons). They were all staring at the hairdryer. I could sense their fear.

'What exactly do you intend to do with that?' asked Glob.

'I'll ... I'll ... shoot you! If you don't release Planet Earth immediately.'

'I've already told you, I can't stop the planet from being recycled,' said the captain cautiously. I could tell he was extremely nervous.

'You can, and you WILL!' I yelled. I knew he was telling the truth, but I had run out of options.

'I don't think you will shoot us,' said Glob, who rolled towards me. There was an audible gasp from the rest of the crew.

'Stay back or I WILL shoot!' I said firmly.

'Recycling of planet completion in thirty seconds.'

'Shoot me with what? A hairdryer!' said Glob.

'This isn't a hairdryer, it's a gun!' I said weakly, waving it in the air so they couldn't get a proper look. Then the cable fell out of my bag.

'Nope, it's a hairdryer,' said Glob correctly.

'It isn't even plugged in!' said the captain, trying to act as if he *hadn't* been fooled by it.

'I'll still shoot!' I said desperately, and I began to sweat. This time the captain knew to jump out of the way, but I still managed to spray half the crew.

'Go ahead!' said the captain laughing. 'Here, I'll even plug it in for you.'

'Recycling of planet completion in ten seconds.'

This was it. In just ten seconds' time Chloe's home was going to be destroyed and here I was, the only life form with any chance of saving it, armed with nothing but a hairdryer.

'Nine.' The speakers continued to count down.

I looked at Chloe, who gazed helplessly back at me, her eyes pleading with me to do something, anything, to save her home.

'Eight.'

I looked at Tanka, who was a sea of pent-up rage. She continued to shout as the seconds ticked away to try and assert her authority, but the captain ignored her protests, unaware that he was speaking to the ACTUAL Queen of the Universe.

'Seven.'

'Go ahead, blast us with hot air!' said the captain, laughing at me.

'Six.'

A hairdryer. That's ALL I had.

'Five.'

Then I remembered, this wasn't any ORDINARY hairdryer. It was a *Vansarian*-powered hairdryer.

'**Four.**'

Inspiration struck. I pulled out a jar of gloop.

'**Three.**'

'Mylan, careful!' said Tanka. I opened the lid and chucked the contents high into the air.

'**Two.**'

I looked at Planet Earth one last time.

'**One.**'

I aimed the hairdryer at the gloop, closed my eyes and blasted it towards Earth at full power.

'**Zero. Recycling of planet complete.**'

PLANETARY PINEAPPLES

I took a breath, then opened my eyes.

Planet Earth was gone.

It had been replaced with a giant pineapple.

'What just happened? Where's Earth?' said Chloe, speaking on behalf of everyone on the captain's deck, who were looking at the giant pineapple with zunkingly confused faces. The guards let go of her in the confusion and she got to her feet.

I smiled. It had worked; it had ACTUALLY worked.

'Right there,' I said, pointing at the pineapple.

'Where? Behind that pineapple?!' said Chloe, trying to look round the side of the inexplicably large fruit.

'Nope. It IS the pineapple,' said
Tanka, taking my hand. 'Well done,
Mylan. Brilliant work. So clever!'

I was being praised by the Queen of the
Universe! I'd thought her cutting my hair was
the best feeling ever! It was nothing compared to
this.

'You turned my planet into a pineapple?!' Chloe
screamed, assuming I had done something pretty
stupid again.

'Look closer,' I said.

Chloe focused on the pineapple. I could see her look up at the laser and then she began to put it together.

'The red mist is gone,' she said thoughtfully. 'And it's been replaced by a sort of gloopy texture ... That's Earth! The gloop changed its appearance and tricked the machine into thinking there wasn't a planet there!' Chloe jumped up and down. 'Oh, Mylan, you did it, you saved Earth!' She threw herself into my arms. I thought her hopelessness was the most powerful feeling I had ever felt, but in that moment I learnt joy is way more powerful than any other feeling. We leapt around in glee.

'Glob, why is there some sort of strange, spiky spaceship where the planet was?' said the captain, who had not been listening to us. He had been staring intently at the pineapple, trying to figure out what it was.

'I'm not sure,' said Glob, looking at a computer screen. 'It says the planet has been recycled but I have never seen this side effect before.'

'What did you do?!' shouted the captain at me.

'What did HE do?! What about everything YOU

did!' said Chloe, who this time managed to reach the captain and she stamped hard on his foot. The guards pulled her away, but not before she had the satisfaction of seeing him hopping in pain and yelling furiously.

At this moment I realised that the captain had no idea what had happened or that Earth was still on his ship. Chloe attacking him only helped confirm in his mind he had successfully destroyed Earth. I took advantage of this by shouting, 'It's a bomb!', turning to wink at Tanka and Chloe.

'What?!' said the captain.

'A bomb. You know, to blow your ship up,' I said, looking at him as if he was stupid.

The guards who had grabbed Chloe let go of her immediately and ran for their lives.

'But ... why?!' said the captain.

'Punishment!' declared Tanka. 'I told you, I am the Queen of the Universe. You just destroyed a planet that was under MY protection, so now we are going to destroy your ship.' She took hold of the hairdryer.

'But that's just a hairdryer, and you aren't REALLY

Tanka Tanka Woo Woo,' said Glob.

The captain walked over and wiped Tanka's face, expecting to get a handful of gloop. He didn't, and he went white with fear.

'But ... you're ... Tanka ...'

'Your Royal Highness to you,' she said.

'And that means that must be ...' said the captain, pointing at the hairdryer.

'Vansarian Tech, able to create bombs out of thin air, and that one there is set to explode in five minutes,' said Tanka regally.

'No, please!' said the captain, dropping to his knees. Glob rolled over and buried his face in the ground.

'We'll do anything. Please just stop the bomb, I'm begging you!' said the captain.

'We'd LOVE to,' said Chloe, strolling over with a glint in her eye. 'Problem is, once the timer is set, it's simply IMPOSSIBLE to switch off. I mean, the paperwork alone ...' She had to stifle a laugh when she said this.

'Right, best be off,' I said, giving the captain a salute.

'But what about us?' said the captain, looking at us

in desperation.

'Oh, don't worry, it's pretty simple. Step one, get off this spaceship.'

'And step two?' asked Glob.

'It's a one-step plan,' I said with a smile.

I headed over to the control panel and pressed the big red button, and we began to travel back down towards our spaceship, *Rusty*. We were all laughing as we got on board, but then Chloe suddenly stopped, the smile vanishing from her face as she went a ghostly white.

'WAIT! What about Earth? They might not know it, but it's STILL on their ship!'

I smiled. 'For now, but do you really think they will keep what they think is a giant bomb on their ship for long?'

'Of course! As soon as we leave, they'll just release it!'

'Exactly,' I said.

And that is what happened. No sooner had we flown out of *The Spaceship* than we saw a giant pineapple glide out of the back of it. Moments later, our speaker systems were taken over by the captain.

'HA! Bet you didn't see that coming, did you! Thought we would just abandon our ship, scared of a little bomb. NOPE! Easy as opening up the back door and – WHOOSH, out it goes!'

'So they COULD have let Earth go all this time! What a bunch of skonkle plops!' said Chloe angrily. I was impressed; she was picking up space lingo nicely.

'I guess we win this round. Sorry about your stinking little planet! BYEEEEEEE!' said the captain as *The Spaceship* zoomed out of sight.

'ARRGH!' screamed Chloe in frustration.

'What's wrong?' I said, putting an arm round her.

'I'm sorry,' said Chloe, giving me a hug. 'I'm so happy that Earth is saved. I'm just annoyed that the captain thinks he got the better of us, even if he didn't. Is that stupid?'

'Not at all,' I said, squeezing her gently.

'Don't worry,' said Tanka, taking both of us by the hand. 'Do you really think I would let them go? I put a tracking device on their ship. Vansarian Tech, of course, so completely undetectable. As soon as I have powered up my own ship I will track them down, with my Vansarian friends, and put a stop to ULRA once and for all. Besides, you did give him a piece of your mind. Bet that felt good!'

'It really did!' said Chloe with a beaming smile.

'Thank you, Your Royal Highness,' I said.

'Please, call me Tanka,' she said, giving my hand a squeeze. 'What you did back there, when we were seconds away from disaster, was brave. Stupid, but zunking brave, and just a little bit clever too.'

Chloe walked over to the window.

'All those people saved ...' she mused, looking at the pineapple. 'Although, any chance you could stop it looking like that?'

'Don't worry, the gloop's power will run out in a few hours and the people down there will have absolutely no idea that to passing space folk they look like a giant pineapple.'

'NASA's satellites might be in for a bit of a shock,' said Chloe. I laughed, but I had no idea what she was talking about.

'So I can go home?' said Chloe.

'You can,' I said with relief.

'And where will you go?' Chloe asked me.

I paused for a second and took a deep breath. 'I need to collect *Old Faithful* and then go home myself,' I said, looking out at the stars. 'I need to convince my fellow Empathians to join me in helping the Universe.'

'Do you think they will believe you?' said Chloe, knowing the difficulty I faced.

'I don't know. Empathians are fiercely loyal to my parents and will struggle to believe they lied to them, but if I don't try, I will never know. I have more than enough stories to share, and this one – well, this tops the lot!'

'Maybe we can do better than just a story,' said Chloe.

'I agree,' said Tanka with a firm nod.

'What do you mean?' I asked, genuinely confused.

Chloe and Tanka looked at each other and smiled.

'You don't seriously think we're letting you go home on your own, do you?' said Chloe.

RETURN TO EMPATHIA

The journey back to Empathia whizzed by in a
heartbeat. Turns out time moves more quickly when
you're with friends.

'Is that it?' asked Tanka, pointing out the window of
Old Faithful at my home planet.

'That's it,' I said warmly.

'It's ... lovely,' she said, clearly unimpressed with my
tiny, insignificant planet. At least she tried to hide it
though, which was kind; not that she could hide it
from an Empathian.

'I'm nervous,' I said, staring longingly at the planet
I had been away from for so long. It felt good to be

home, but at the same time I was terrified. I kept thinking, what if no one believed me? I would feel awful, but then I would think, what if they DO believe me and realise my parents had LIED? I would still feel terrible.

'You can do this, Mylan,' said Tanka, rubbing my shoulders.

'Doing the right thing is never easy, but it's the right thing to do,' said Chloe.

She was right. Doing the right thing was *the right thing*. I nodded and steered *Old Faithful* towards the surface of Empathia.

The door opened and, for the first time in for ever, I set foot on Empathia. I knelt on the ground and kissed it.

'Home,' I said, and a tear formed in my eye.

'Wow, Mylan, your planet is incredible!' said Chloe. 'It smells just like candyfloss! I love the red sea. And the trees sing so beautifully. It really is Zoop, Zap, Zop.' She wasn't as well travelled as the Queen of the Universe and, other than Earth, the only planets she had been on were full of 480-year-old poop or hairdressing salons, but I could tell she really meant it. That meant a lot to me.

I took in a deep breath of the candyfloss-scented Empathian air, filling my lungs to the brim, then I let out a long, huge sigh. I stood up, and that was the first time I noticed that something wasn't quite right.

It was quiet. WAY too quiet. I knew it would be, because compared to any other planet where I would get overwhelmed by life forms' problems, a Utopia like Empathia was going to be a calming place.

But I could barely feel anything at all, which was never usually the case. I began to panic a little, desperately searching for signs of life. Then, in the silence, I felt something incredibly strong. It was as if the planet was speaking to me itself. It was a message of love.

I began running through the fields that I raced through as a kid, weaving in and out of the trees as they sang. They were singing one word over and over. 'Home.'

I was practically at a sprint now and behind me I could hear the distant shouts of Tanka and Chloe as they tried to keep up, unsure of what was happening.

I ran down a steep bank and was surprised when I hit the bottom to land in a lake. It wasn't there last time I was here, so it was a pretty big surprise, and it was a pretty big lake. Even stranger, the water wasn't red. It was a light shade of blue.

I thrashed around a little and got a mouthful of water. I spat it out immediately. Instead of it tasting of sweet cranberry juice, it was salty. I dipped back under the water and then a hand reached in and grabbed me, pulling me on to the bank of yellow earth. It was my dad.

'SON!' he said, grabbing hold of me as tightly as he could.

'Is it him? Is it really our darling boy?' said my mum, who leapt on top of me. Her grip was even tighter than my dad's. I could feel their delight and love.

'It's so good to see you!' I said. Despite the fact they had lied to our entire planet and I had set off on a quest to expose them, I still loved them dearly. After all, they were my mum and dad. And they meant well.

'Even better to see you, Mylan. I LOVE your hair!' said my mum, wrapping me up in her arms once more.

At this point, Tanka Tanka Woo Woo and Chloe caught up with us.

'Is that ...' said my dad, pointing at Tanka Tanka Woo Woo.

'The Queen of the Universe. Yes,' said Tanka plainly.

My mum jumped up and did a weird mix of a curtsey and a bow. What was even weirder was my dad tried to do the same thing. Being royalty themselves, they had never had to bow or curtsey to anyone before and they had no idea what to do. It was also clear that they had never met her before. That had been a lie too.

As they fumbled over each other, trying to pay their respects to Tanka, I stood up and steadied myself, remembering the reason I had returned home.

'Mum, Dad ... You know why I am here,' I said in the most authoritative voice I could muster. Chloe laughed, which really didn't help.

'Oh, Mylan, we know …' said my mum, turning to face me.

'You're here to tell everyone that we lied. That the Universe is a place in tremendous trouble,' said my dad.

'No offence, Your Royal Highness. I'm sure you are doing a wonderful job,' added my mum quickly.

'Oh, yes, wonderful job indeed,' my dad added. 'But you're too late, Mylan. I'm afraid there is no one left to tell.'

That's why it was so quiet. I could feel it now; my parents were the only Empathians left on the planet. A horrible feeling emerged in my stomach as I struggled to think what had happened to my home.

'We told them!' screamed my mum, bursting into tears.

'Almost as soon as you left,' added my dad. 'You have to understand, Mylan, we felt zunking terrible about lying to everyone, but we thought it was for the greater good.'

Tanka stepped forward, clearly not impressed by the 'greater good' line, but I raised my hand to stop her and, to my surprise, she did.

'But losing you over it … The pain was unbearable, Mylan,' said my mum.

'And of course on Empathia, everyone felt that pain too!' said Chloe. I smiled at her; she really was a smart cookie. She would do well as an intergalactic traveller.

'Yes, quite right. A mother's love is impossible to hide,' said my mum, also impressed.

'Despite all our efforts, Empathia became just as bad as any other planet we visited. Everyone was so miserable that we decided to come clean. We told everyone the truth, and it hurt. It really hurt,' said my dad, wiping away a tear.

'The entire planet cried for three straight days. So much so, this lake formed from the tears. We called it Lake Mylan,' said my mum. It explained why the water was so salty and blue. Empathian tears were particularly salty.

'So what happened?' I said, eager to know.

'When everyone realised that there were people out in the Universe in pain that needed help, they did what any good Empathian would do,' said my dad.

'They left. They did exactly what you did, Mylan; what we were too afraid to do because we are TERRIBLE Empathians.' My mum burst into tears, which set off the entire planet. Well, me, my dad, Chloe and Tanka, which amounted to the same thing.

'You're not terrible Empathians, you just made a mistake. Trust me, I've made a few of my own ...' I said.

'Yeah, don't let him order ice cream for you,' said Chloe. I shot her a disapproving look with my eyes, but my mouth couldn't help but form a little smile.

'Oh, Mylan, we are so sorry and we will never, ever forgive ourselves!' said my dad.

'Then perhaps I can help,' said Tanka, putting her arms around my parents. 'As Queen of the Universe, I hereby forgive you for any wrongdoings against the planet of Empathia.' Tanka clapped above their heads and then splashed them with her hair. I was pretty sure she was making up the ritual, but I appreciated the effort.

'Um ... can you really do that?' asked my mum.

'I'm the Queen of the Universe. Of course I can,' said Tanka with a smile.

'But we lied to so many people ...'

'As your son said, everyone makes mistakes. Except me, of course,' said Tanka, winking at Chloe. 'But there is one thing you did that was right, very right indeed. Raising your son. This young man helped me bring down an evil organisation, saving countless planets and all the lives within them. You should be zunking proud to have raised such a Zoop, Zap, Zop boy.'

'Wow! We are. We really are so proud of you, Mylan,' said my mum, hugging me once more. We cried some more and held each other tight. After an incredibly long hug, a question formed in my head.

'So there's really no one left?' I asked, looking around.

'No, it's been just us for a very long time. We only stayed because we hoped that one day you would return,' said my dad.

'Well, here I am,' I said cheerfully.

'Here you are,' said my mum.

'Then I guess you have nothing left to stay here for,

and there sure are a few planets out there that could use our help,' I said, before looking at Chloe. 'Right after we drop you off on Earth, of course, Chloe!'

Chloe came over and gave me a hug.

'Absolutely. Although, perhaps we could do a little bit of exploring on the way?' she added with a cheeky grin.

'Sure, why not,' I said, before taking my rucksack off my back. I reached in and pulled out the book I had been writing for over a thousand years.

I read the title out loud.

'The Worst Days Ever! By Mylan Bletzleburger.' And placed it on the ground.

'What is that?' my mum asked.

'It's a long story,' I said. 'But a tale that's over now.'

'Are you sure? You have spent so long collecting and writing those stories. Are you really going to just leave that book here?' asked Chloe.

'I'm done with bad days,' I said with a smile. 'My next book ... I'm going to focus on the good ones.'

'HILARIOUS AND SO SILLY!'
TOM FLETCHER

ONE BOY. ONE DISAPPOINTING SUPERPOWER.

IGUANA BOY

SAVES THE WORLD WITH A TRIPLE CHEESE PIZZA

JAMES BISHOP illustrated by RIKIN PAREKH

DYLAN, AKA **IGUANA BOY**, IS READY FOR HIS **FIRST DAY** AT **SUPERHERO HQ.**

BUT INSTEAD OF BEING SENT ON **SUPER-COOL MISSIONS**, HE'S PLACED IN THE CITD ... THE CATS IN TREES DEPARTMENT.

LUCKILY, SUPERVILLAIN **REPEAT OFFENDER** IS ROBBING **BANK** AFTER **BANK**.

CAN **IGUANA BOY** BECOME THE **FIRST SUPERHERO EVER** TO STOP REPEAT OFFENDER IN 30 SECONDS **OR LESS?**

DYLAN, AKA **IGUANA BOY**, IS EPICALLY FAILING HIS **SUPERHERO MISSIONS.**

FORTUNATELY, A **MYSTERIOUS HERO** IS ABOUT TO TURN HIS **LUCK** AROUND ...

THEN SUPERVILLAIN **MIND BENDER** KIDNAPS **ALL** THE SUPERHEROES, AND DEMANDS THE GOVERNMENT WORK **FLAT OUT** ON A SPECIAL **GOLDEN TOOTHBRUSH!**

CAN IGUANA BOY SAVE THE DAY, ALONE? (WITH THE HELP OF HIS TRUSTY IGUANAS!)